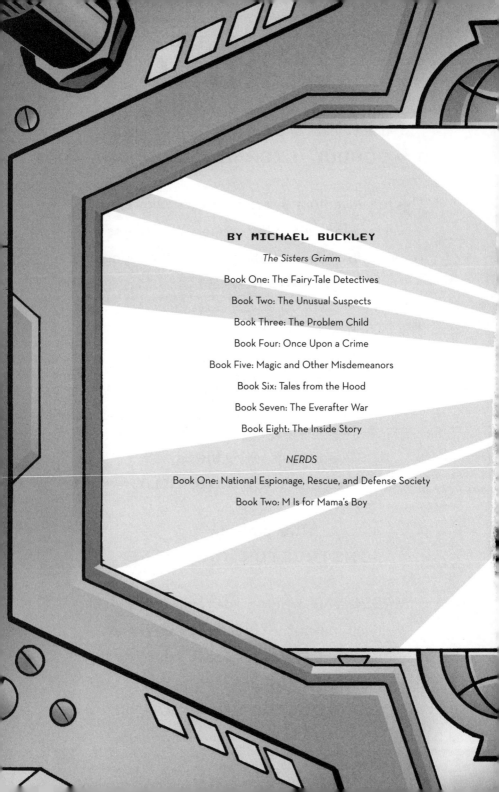

BY MICHAEL BUCKLEY

The Sisters Grimm

NERDS

For dorks, dweebs,
geeks, spazzes,
waste cases, and
nerds everywhere.
Someday you too
will change the
world.

TOP SECRET!

THIS BOOK IS A NERDS CASE FILE. IT
CONTAINS HIGHLY SENSITIVE MATERIAL
AND WAS COMPILED FROM THE SWORN
TESTIMONIES OF EYEWITNESSES. IT ALSO
CONTAINS INFORMATION RETRIEVED FROM
INTERROGATIONS AND CONFESSIONS.

WHAT I'M TRYING TO SAY, KID, IS DON'T
LOSE IT! IF THE INFORMATION IN THIS BOOK
FELL INTO THE WRONG HANDS, IT WOULD
CAUSE A NATIONAL SECURITY CRISIS.
SO DO US ALL A FAVOR AND DON'T SHOW
THIS BOOK TO ANYONE.

HOW DO I HAVE ACCESS TO THIS
INFORMATION?

WELL, I USED TO BE A MEMBER OF NERDS—
BACK WHEN I WAS YOUR AGE. IT'S TRUE! MY
CODE NAME WAS BEANPOLE. WHAT ARE YOU
LAUGHING AT? BEANPOLE IS A GREAT SECRET
AGENT NAME. ANYWAY, NOW THAT I'M OLDER, MY
JOB IS TO DOCUMENT THE AGENTS AND THEIR
MISSIONS. TECHNICALLY, NOW THAT I'VE TOLD
YOU ALL OF THIS, I'M SUPPOSED TO KILL
YOU, BUT YOU LOOK LIKE A GOOD ENOUGH
PERSON. BESIDES, THE TEAM THINKS YOU HAVE
POTENTIAL. IN FACT, THEY ARE CONSIDERING
YOU FOR A SPOT. BUT FIRST WE NEED TO MAKE
SURE YOU'RE UP TO THE CHALLENGE. READ THIS
BOOK FROM COVER TO COVER, AND IF AT THE
END YOU THINK YOU'VE GOT WHAT IT TAKES . . .
WELL, LET'S NOT GET AHEAD OF OURSELVES.
YOU'VE GOT TO READ IT FIRST.

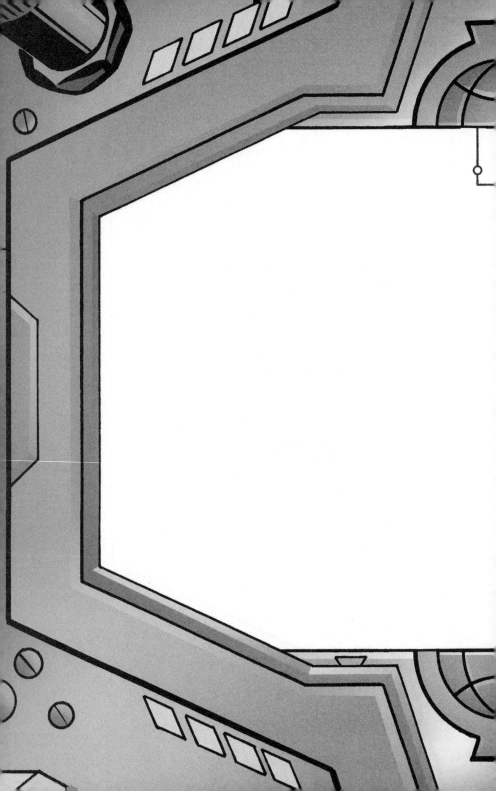

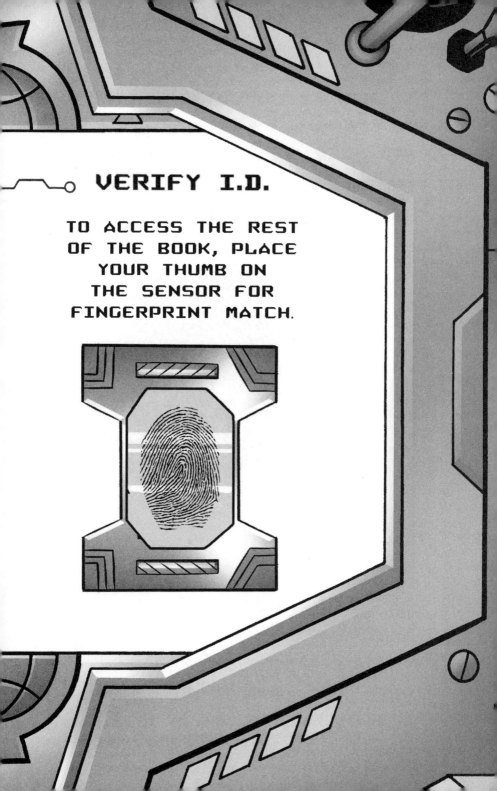

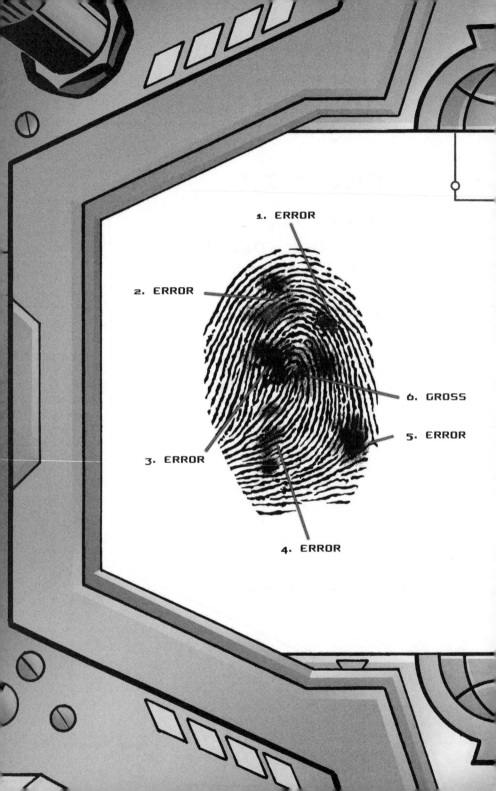

The Library of Congress has cataloged the hardcover edition of this book as follows:

Buckley, Michael.
NERDS : National Espionage, Rescue, and Defense Society / by Michael Buckley.
p. cm. — (NERDS ; bk. 1)
Summary: While running a spy network from their elementary school,
five socially awkward misfits combine their talents and use cutting-edge
gadgetry to fight evil around the world.
ISBN 978-0-8109-4324-7
[1. Spies—Fiction. 2. Schools—Fiction. 3. Humorous stories.] I. Title. II. Title:
National Espionage, Rescue, and Defense Society.
PZ7.B882323Ne 2009
[Fic]—dc22
2009015484

Paperback ISBN 978-0-8109-8985-6

Text copyright © 2010 Michael Buckley
Illustrations copyright © 2010 Ethen Beavers
Book design by Chad W. Beckerman

Printed and bound in U.S.A.
10 9 8 7 6 5 4 3 2 1

ABRAMS
THE ART OF BOOKS SINCE 1949

115 West 18th Street
New York, NY 10011
www.abramsbooks.com

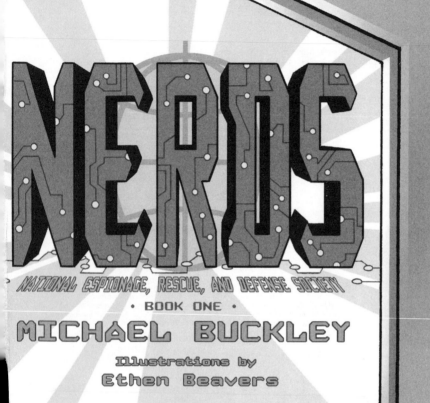

NERDS

NATIONAL ESPIONAGE, RESCUE, AND DEFENSE SOCIETY

· BOOK ONE ·

MICHAEL BUCKLEY

Illustrations by Ethen Beavers

AMULET BOOKS

NEW YORK

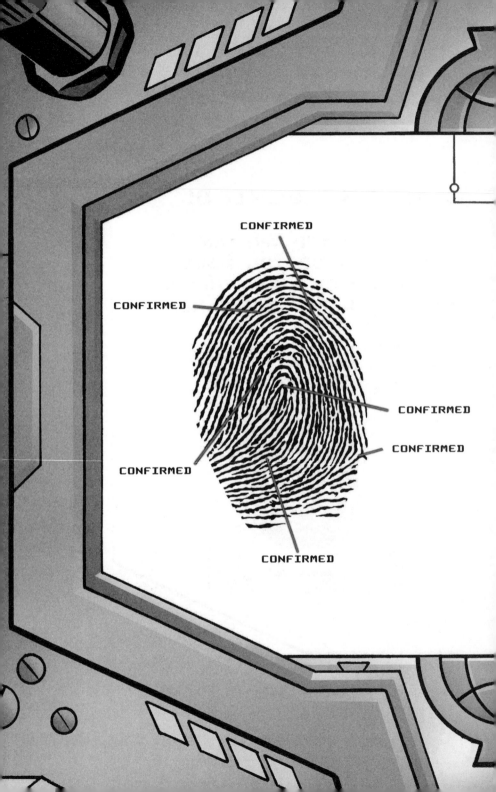

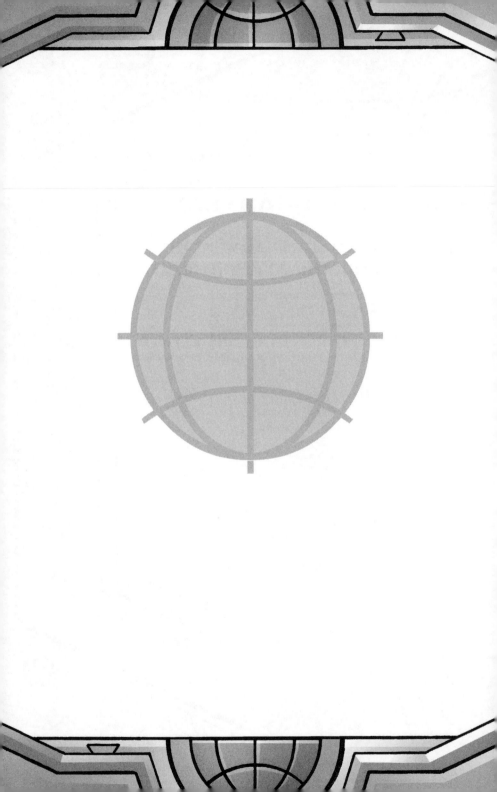

PROLOGUE

Alexander Brand was a secret agent. He had saved the world on more than a dozen occasions. He had stopped three invasions of the United States by foreign powers. He had helped depose six dictators and four corrupt presidents. He had a bevy of skills that served him well, including: defusing land mines, driving tanks, parachuting into hostile territories, infiltrating terrorist compounds, wearing disguises, engaging in underwater hand-to-hand combat, and breaking codes. Plus, he looked awesome in a tuxedo. At one time, Brand was the United States' most valuable spy. But that was before the accident.

"I heard about the accident," General Savage said as he glanced over his desk at the white cane resting on Brand's lap. The cane was an ugly thing to Savage—like a rattlesnake. It made him uncomfortable, and when he was uncomfortable

Savage lost his temper. He slammed his hand down on his desk, and considering the size of his hand, it was a wonder the desk didn't crack in two. The general was a mountain of muscles with a tree trunk–size neck and a face like a slab of concrete. He'd fought in fourteen wars. Rumor had it that he'd started ten of them himself just to stay in practice.

Brand nodded respectfully. He didn't want to talk about the explosion that had injured his leg. He wasn't the talking type. He could dismantle, clean, and rebuild an AK-47 in forty-two seconds, but share his feelings? Never tried it.

"Well, I have something that will put a smile on your face," Savage said as he opened a drawer in his desk and pulled out an overstuffed manila folder with the words TOP SECRET printed on it in red. He passed it to the former spy and sat back in his chair with a knowing grin. "I was wondering if you are ready to get back to work."

Agent Brand ran his hand across the folder's crimson warning. The words "top secret" always sent a spark of excitement through him. He loved secrets. Codes, puzzles, mysteries—they seemed to run through his veins. Still, he resisted the temptation to open the folder. What was the point?

"Sir, I appreciate the offer. Nothing would make me happier than serving my country, but I'm not interested in a desk job. I won't push papers, not even for Uncle Sam." Brand set the folder on Savage's desk and grasped his cane, ready to leave.

"Just take a look, agent," the general said. "This isn't a desk job."

Brand opened the folder and scanned the top page. The man who had seen everything couldn't believe his eyes.

"I thought these guys were a myth," Brand whispered.

"That's how we like to keep it. Even the president is in the dark."

"You're keeping this from the commander in chief?"

Savage wiped sweat from his forehead with his sleeve. "Their work is too important. We can't let anyone distract them."

"So you want me to join them?" Brand asked.

"Not exactly," Savage said. "Turn the page."

Brand did as he was instructed. The next page did not make him happy.

"They're not spies. They're—"

"They're the world's last, best hope, Agent Brand. When the best of the best can't get it done, we send these guys. They have billions of dollars of technology at their fingertips, and the perfect cover. We can drop them pretty much anywhere and they go virtually undetected. You have no idea the debt the world owes them. The team is young, inexperienced, and now drifting without a rudder. Their last director died under mysterious circumstances. He jumped out a window."

"Spy jobs are stressful, General. There's nothing mysterious about that," Brand said.

"I would agree, except the window overlooked the shark tank at the local aquarium," Savage said.

"Hmmm," the spy replied.

"And he had a bomb strapped to his chest and three knives in his back."

"That does raise a few eyebrows," Brand said. "Still, General, what you're describing to me is a glorified baby-sitting job."

Savage shook his head. "You're not getting it, Brand. This is a chance to get our best team back under control. I'm sorry it's not sports cars and exotic women, but it's a way to get back into the game."

Just then there was a knock at the general's door. A nervous little man with short red hair and a face full of freckles poked his head into the room. "General, I'm sorry to interrupt—"

"This better be good, Casey! I told you not to bother me."

"We have a crisis," Casey said. "It's Greenland."

"Who is Greenland?"

"Greenland isn't a who, sir. It's a place." Casey swallowed hard, as if afraid to correct his boss. "It's the world's largest island. It's off the coast of North America, very close to—"

Savage pounded his hand on the desk once more. This time one of the legs broke, and the desk tilted so that the general's work slid off. "I know where Greenland is! What about it?"

"It just slammed into Iceland," Casey said.

"It what?" Agent Brand asked.

"It collided with Iceland," Casey said.

"How does something like that happen?" Brand asked.

"W-we're not sure, sir," the assistant stammered.

"Scramble the team," the general barked. "Someone is behind this! Giant islands don't just move around by themselves."

Casey nodded and dashed away.

"What do you say, Agent Brand? Can America count on its bravest secret agent again?" the general asked as he turned his attention to a globe of the Earth still teetering on the edge of his desk.

The spy nodded. "I'm in."

The general smiled. "Good. Now, let's talk about your cover."

1

Jackson Jones peered through his binoculars at the horizon. He spotted his targets climbing the crest of an embankment not more than a quarter of a mile away. He smiled and turned to his partner and friend, Brett Bealer. "They're coming."

Brett nodded, then turned to signal to the rest of Jackson's team. They scampered into position behind shrubberies, trees, and lampposts. They were practically invisible to the enemy.

Jackson's team was eager, but their leader knew that surprising the enemy required patience. They would have one chance, and if they blew it, weeks of planning would be wasted.

Though he would never admit it to the others, Jackson found the enemy unnerving. They were grotesque with their drooling mouths and puffy eyes—barely human. Brett was convinced the enemy had been born misshapen, but the idea was far too unsettling for Jackson. He couldn't imagine being born a . . . a . . . a nerd.

Unfortunately for Jackson, Nathan Hale Elementary had more than its fair share of nerds. In fact, his whole town of Arlington, Virginia, was one giant geektropolis. Perhaps there was something in the drinking water Arlington siphoned from the Potomac River, but there were dweebs, spazzes, goobers, gomers, goofballs, and freak-outs crawling out of every nook and cranny. Jackson sometimes felt as if he were drowning in an ocean of wheezing, math-loving, Velcro sneaker–wearing waste cases. Jackson's high school–age brother, Chaz, felt the same way. He told Jackson the elementary school had always been overrun with misfits. Their father, who was also an alumnus of Nathan Hale, said the same. Jackson was smack-dab in the middle of Nerdville, USA.

Jackson heard the honking of someone blowing his nose and he knew the enemy had arrived. He peeked out from his hiding spot and saw them stumbling up the sidewalk toward the school. It was time for action.

"Attack!"

His signal sent the nerds scattering like frightened cattle. They bayed and bellowed and rushed about, knocking into one another.

"First wave!" Jackson cried, and his team removed

drinking straws from their pockets. They loaded the straws with sticky-wet spitballs and aimed them at the panicked nerds. "Fire at will!"

A wave of spitwads blasted through the air, raining down on the geeks. One kid with exceptionally large buck teeth was blinded when a dozen sloppy wads hit him in the face. He ran headfirst into a flagpole and knocked himself unconscious.

"Leave us alone!" a girl shouted in a wheezy voice as she was peppered with sticky ammunition.

Before the nerds could peel the gooey missiles off their faces and clothes, Jackson called for the second wave of attacks. The straws were tossed aside, and his team pounced on the misfits; administering purple nurples, blistering pink bellies, cruel charley horses, and nasty noogies. Ears were flicked. Wet willies were delivered. KICK ME signs were applied to unsuspecting backs.

Everything was going according to plan, but Jackson was determined not to get lazy. He called for the third and final wave, the part of the plan they called "the hammer." They spun the geeks around, grabbed the backs of their underpants, and yanked toward the heavens. The elastic waistbands were then pulled over the victims' heads. Atomic wedgies. The final, crushing blow.

The nerds flopped around on the ground like fish, trying

unsuccessfully to stuff their underwear back into their pants. Jackson, Brett, and the others celebrated their success.

Now, to the casual observer, Jackson would appear to be a jerk, but in fact he was very popular. Very, very, very, very, very, very, very, very, very popular. His teachers described him as charming. He was captain of his PeeWee football team, and his coach said Jackson had the best passing arm, best kicking leg, and best touchdown dance he had seen in twenty-five years. Kids copied Jackson's every move, hung on his every word. Even some of the teachers started to dress like him.

Yes, Jackson Jones was blessed, but little did he know that the cruel hand of fate was about to smack him in the face, and it would all start with a single word.

"Interesting."

"Whaghh?" Jackson asked. He would have been clearer but he was sitting in his orthodontist's office with a suction tube in his mouth. Dr. Gupta, who had said the word, was looking at his teeth.

Jackson knew it was never a good sign when a medical professional used the word "interesting." It was one of those words you never wanted to hear a doctor say, like "rare," "inoperable," and "flesh-eating."

"Very interesting," the orthodontist chirped as he continued his examination.

"Whaghh?" Jackson cried.

Dr. Gupta was too excited to speak. In his twenty years as an orthodontist, he had heard many medical-phenomenon stories. The podiatrist in suite 4A had a patient with eight toes on each foot. His brother-in-law, an emergency-room doctor, claimed to have had a patient with a third eye. Even his dog's veterinarian, Dr. Hanger, had a two-headed turtle under his care. Now Gupta had his *own* medical oddity. He crossed the room to a telephone, picked it up, and punched in a number. "Donna, can you bring the camera in here?"

A moment later a pale, sleepy woman entered the room. Dr. Gupta directed her to look into Jackson's open mouth. Her drowsy eyelids popped open.

Dr. Gupta clapped his hands like a happy baby. "I know, right? No one will believe it if we don't take some pictures."

"Whhhaaaaaagggggghhhh?" Jackson cried, but again he was ignored.

Donna snapped pictures from various angles. The camera's flash blinded Jackson, and by the time the blue and red spots disappeared from his vision, his patience was gone. He yanked the suction tube from his mouth. "What's going on?"

Dr. Gupta smiled as he rubbed his hands together. "Well, Jackson, how do I explain this? It's just . . . well, a normal person has twenty-eight teeth. Some have several more if they still have their wisdom teeth. You, however, have a lot more."

"How many?"

Dr. Gupta smiled. "You have sixty-four teeth! In fact, you have four rows of them, two on the top and two on the bottom."

"Is that unusual?" Jackson asked.

"Not if you're a great white shark," the doctor replied, handing Jackson a mirror so that he could take a look for himself.

Jackson studied his mouth closely. Besides remembering to brush, he had never given much thought to his teeth. He assumed everyone had as many as he did, though he recalled his father complaining just last week that the family was spending a fortune on dental floss. "So, what are you going to do about it? I can't walk around with this many teeth."

"Well, we'll have to extract those extra choppers."

"Extract?"

"Yeah. You know, yank them out. But there is good news. The tooth fairy is going to owe you a bundle."

Gupta slapped his knee and burst into a giggling fit. After a while he wiped the happy tears from his cheeks. "Sorry, that's an old orthodontist joke."

"Is it going to hurt?" Jackson asked.

"Absolutely. But that's not even your biggest problem. You've got summer teeth."

"What are 'summer teeth'?"

"Sum 'er going this way and sum 'er going that way," Dr. Gupta said, chuckling. He wondered if perhaps a career in stand-up comedy had been his true calling.

Jackson, however, was not amused, and when Gupta spotted his scowl, the orthodontist got back to business. "Sorry. What I'm trying to say is your teeth are all over the place. A few of them are sideways. There's one that's upside-down! Don't worry. It's nothing a set of braces won't fix."

Jackson felt his heart stop. "Braces!" *Nerds* had braces.

Dr. Gupta smiled reassuringly. "A lot of patients worry that braces are going to ruin their lives, but I assure you that nothing will change, Jackson. Your friends are still going to like you. I doubt that anyone will notice at all."

When Jackson looked back on that moment, he realized that was when a terrible truth was revealed to him: Adults are liars, horrible, soulless, black-hearted liars. The braces didn't just ruin his life, they demolished it, then salted the land so nothing would ever grow there again! When Dr. Gupta was finished, Jackson was thirty-two teeth lighter but fourteen pounds of metal heavier. Each of his teeth was encased in a jagged steel cage that ripped at his gums. Worse, a metal halo that Gupta called "headgear" was attached to Jackson's bicuspids, and protruded out of his mouth and encircled his head like Saturn's rings.

It also turned out to be highly magnetic.

Jackson found that by the end of an average school day, his headgear had collected cuff links, belt buckles, hairpins, cafeteria trays, cell phones, and umbrellas. He once stepped too close to a school bus and became locked onto its bumper. He was helplessly dragged through a rainstorm as children were dropped off all over town. He nearly died the night his father decided to treat the family to dinner at the local hibachi restaurant.

But the most horrible side effect he suffered wasn't the pain or the humiliation—it was the sudden end to his reign as king of Nathan Hale Elementary. His popularity vanished overnight. Friends turned their backs when he walked by. Teachers cowered in the lounge, hoping to avoid eye contact. The classroom hamster buried itself under a mound of sawdust and pretended he wasn't there. Even his best friend turned on him.

"Nice braces, goober," Brett said when Jackson tried to sit at their usual lunch table. "You look like you've been munching on a bicycle chain." Their other friends laughed and refused to let Jackson sit down. They banished him to a table in the far corner of the cafeteria where even the custodian with the lazy eye wouldn't go.

His brother, Chaz, was even crueler. He called Jackson

"Braceface" and "Nerdatron." (Chaz had a thing for robot humor.) He found particular amusement in Jackson's headgear. At dinnertime, Chaz would bring a collection of household tools with him to see which would snap off the table and attach itself to Jackson's face. In the night he snuck into Jackson's room and strung party balloons to it. When he was suiting up for football practice, Chaz would hang his cleats from it. When Jackson complained to his father, his dad told him to suck it up. "A little ribbing is good for you. It will make you a man."

As the winds of autumn arrived and leaves turned yellow, orange, and red, Jackson sensed the coming of football season and a change in his fortunes. Football was Jackson's last hope for regaining some of his popularity. He was still the team's star quarterback, even if he did have an Erector set circling his head. Sadly, on the first day of practice, Jackson discovered his headgear prevented him from putting on his helmet.

"You can't play without a helmet, kid," the coach said. "You'll get brain damage."

Getting booted off the football team was the last nail in the popularity coffin. Friendless, Jackson drifted through the halls flashing smiles that were never returned, raising his hand for high fives that never came, waiting by his locker for admirers who never showed up. It was as if the warm golden glow that had shined on Jackson his whole life had been turned off.

One day he found himself reminiscing at photos in the school's trophy case—photos of his father leading the Tigers to victory, of his brother catching a touchdown pass. He found a photo of his own team, and saw himself proudly holding the winning trophy, the same trophy his father and brother had won. Sports were the glue that held his family together, especially since his mother died. The Jackson family had no patience for losers. They were winners on and off the field. Where did Jackson fit in now?

Just then, there was a terrific crash as the winning trophy was yanked through the display case glass by Jackson's magnetic headgear. It took several teachers a half hour to pry it off his face.

The next day Jackson was banned from reminiscing.

2

The Hyena reached into her pocket and took out a folded note. She double-checked the co-ordinates written inside and frowned. There was no mistake. She was in the right place and there wasn't a living soul in sight. Her mysterious new employer had started off on the wrong foot. It was rude to leave a person waiting in subzero weather at the North Pole! With a sigh, she wondered why criminal masterminds were so obsessed with desolate locations. Couldn't this "Dr. Jigsaw" meet her in Hawaii or the Bahamas? Half of the money she made as a criminal was spent on mittens and long underwear.

Suddenly, she heard a whipping sound above her and looked to the sky. A black helicopter with no identifying marks of any kind hovered overhead and then landed several yards away. She tried to peer through the windows, but they were tinted black. Then the door opened and two men exited the craft. The first was a tall, thin man with bushy white hair and a neatly trimmed goatee. His face was perfect—too perfect—with well-spaced eyes, a long, straight nose, a strong chin, and not a single wrinkle. But another glance said that this man had had a tremendous amount of plastic surgery; his features had been pulled, pushed, and pounded into place. Now, his dark eyes locked onto the Hyena, studying her features as if making plans to rearrange them as well.

The second man was enormous, with slicked-back hair and chiseled cheekbones. He peered at the Hyena beneath heavy brows. "You da Hyena?" he grunted. His voice told her all she needed to know. He was a goon.

"No, I'm at the North Pole 'cause I'm Santa Claus," she replied. She couldn't stand goons. Stupidity was like an art form to them, and this particular goon was clearly the Leonardo da Vinci of goons.

"Dumb" Vinci sneered and turned back to the helicopter. Inside the still-open doorway the Hyena spied a figure dressed all in black. He—or she—turned toward her, revealing a mask with a ghostly skull painted on it. The figure nodded, and on his signal Dumb Vinci handed the Hyena an envelope full of money.

"Who is that?" the Hyena asked.

The first man ignored her question. "My name is Dr. Felix

Jigsaw. I'm the preeminent expert on tectonic movement—"

"Tectonic what?"

"The movement of continents!" said Jigsaw. It was clear he had little patience for people he considered intellectually inferior. "I have a little project I'm working on and I believe you can help."

"What kind of project?" the Hyena asked as she counted the cash inside the envelope.

"I'm going to conquer the world."

The Hyena sighed. If she had a nickel for every criminal mastermind who said he was going to conquer the world, she'd be a very rich assassin. They never succeeded. Still, there was a lot of money in the envelope. If that was his dream, who was she to discourage him? "Sounds good, boss. What do you want me to do?"

Dr. Jigsaw took a piece of yellow paper out of his coat and handed it to the Hyena. She looked it over and smiled. Her career was finally on track.

"Whom should I kill first?" she asked.

Dr. Jigsaw shook his head. "You aren't killing anyone. I want you to kidnap them."

"Kidnap? That's a job for a goon. I'm an assassin," the Hyena said, trying to hand him back the paper.

"You want da money or not?" Dumb Vinci grunted.

The Hyena glanced at the envelope stuffed with cash. Inside was more than ten thousand dollars. She remembered that her subscription to *Tiger Beat* was about to expire . . . and there were those leather boots she had seen at the mall. . . . She stuffed the money into her pocket. "Once I get them, where do I bring them?"

Dr. Jigsaw turned and pointed toward the horizon. It was then that the Hyena noticed a silver fortress in the distance, built on the ice.

She was going to have to stock up on long underwear.

3

Without the gaggle of friends that usually surrounded him, Jackson felt like a ghost—a formless entity that no one could see or hear. He could have worn a clown suit to school or danced Irish jigs with his hair on fire and no one would have batted an eye, not even his old gang. He watched them from afar as they ate their lunches in the cafeteria. When they laughed, he laughed. When they whispered to one another, he imagined being part of their secret.

He was, in a word, pathetic. But it was during these lonely days that Jackson began to notice things about his friends he had never noticed before. For example, Steve Sarver smelled each bite of his food before he ate it. It didn't matter whether he was having egg salad or peanut butter and jelly, he sniffed then chewed. Sniffed, chewed. Sniffed, chewed. Sniffed, chewed.

Ron Schultz limped, favoring his right leg. Lori Baker licked her lips every 2.3 seconds (Jackson timed it). Jenise Corron wouldn't eat peas. Even his former best friend, Brett Bealer, who had once seemed like the coolest kid Jackson knew, had an odd quirk—he skipped when he ran.

As Jackson sat on the school bus one afternoon thinking about some of the quirks he had seen that day, he felt a tingling sensation at the back of his brain. It swept through his whole body and set his imagination on fire. Why did his friends do the things they did? Were they aware of their strange habits? He decided to dedicate himself to unlocking the mystery of their puzzling behavior.

The next day he began his life as a spy in earnest. He eavesdropped on his friends' conversations. He followed them home. He opened their mail. He dug into their trash for clues. Remarkably, no one questioned his activities. No one stopped to ask why he was sorting through disgusting bags of garbage. Jackson was a social outcast, a misfit, a nerd—kids like that were always doing weird things; it hardly deserved attention. Jackson really was like a ghost.

Eventually, he found clues—little scraps of evidence like puzzle pieces. When they were assembled, they created a picture of the person Jackson was watching. Soon, he knew more about his old friends than they knew about themselves. Steve had once had a violent case of food poisoning from some bad clams he had eaten in Playa del Carmen, Mexico; Ron had an ingrown toenail; Lori drank too much cranberry juice, which gave her a bad case of dry mouth; Jenise had once had a pea lodged in her nostril for two weeks; and Brett, well, he just liked to skip.

To his amazement, Jackson realized that all his former friends were misfits too. Each of them had some bizarre habit that could have easily gotten them ostracized . . . if anyone had noticed. But his discovery puzzled Jackson. If *everyone* was an oddball, why had he been singled out as a nerd? Resentment set in, and Jackson contemplated revenge. He considered posting a list of his friends' bizarre tics on every locker in Nathan Hale Elementary. How would Brett and the others like it when they were the objects of ridicule? How would they feel when they had to eat their lunches under the stairs? But something kept Jackson from carrying out his plan. Not loyalty, he realized, but the fact that his "spy" work had been fun. If he was being honest, it was the most fun he had ever had. And if he wanted to do more of it, he couldn't risk exposure.

The problem with mysteries is once they are solved, they become boring. So when Jackson was done with his former friends, he began spying on other students, and then when they got boring, he moved on to the teachers and staff, the PTA, the band director, and even the crossing guard. Soon Jackson had unlocked nearly every secret at Nathan Hale, and worried that he might have to turn to schoolwork to keep himself occupied. But then, like a ray of sunshine from the heavens above, the "nerd herd" stumbled into his life.

They consisted of five of the most awkward kids in the history of fifth grade: Duncan Dewey, a chubby African American kid whose diet consisted entirely of paste; Matilda Choi, a wheezing and gasping Korean American who was never far from her inhalers; Heathcliff Hodges, a freckled kid whose outrageous overbite made him look like a camel; Ruby Peet, a scratching, sniffing, sweating, and swollen collection of allergies; and finally, Julio Escala, otherwise known as "Flinch." Julio was a walking ball of energy spiked by the dozens of cookies, candy bars, and sugary sodas he consumed each day. He was so hyperactive he appeared as a blur.

Jackson had never really noticed these particular nerds before. It was easy to overlook them. The nerd herd never participated in any clubs or sports. They steered clear of social settings like dances and pep rallies. They had no use for other kids—not even other nerds. It boggled Jackson's mind, but it was almost as if the nerd herd didn't *want* to fit in.

When Jackson told his brother about the herd, Chaz bristled. "You sound like you're envious of them."

Though he didn't admit it to Chaz, Jackson realized that

his brother was sort of right. The herd might have been a collection of misshapen goobers, but at least they had each other. They were inseparable, and Jackson longed to have that kind of friendship again. When he realized he was jealous of a bunch of nerds, it was such a shock he accidentally clamped his teeth down on his thumb. His braces locked together like a vice, requiring a visit from the fire department with their "Jaws of Life."

The next day, thumb in a splint, Jackson set out to solve the mystery of the herd. It wasn't easy. He knew close to nothing about them. Besides lactose-free pudding, the only thing that Duncan, Heathcliff, Matilda, Ruby, and Flinch seemed interested in was reading quietly in the library. Jackson had been completely unaware that his school had a library. At first he was dumbfounded that anyone would want to spend their free time around so many books, but then he spotted the school's librarian, Ms. Holiday. She was an angel in a cardigan sweater. She had blonde hair, skin like milk, and smart-looking glasses that magnified her gorgeous blue eyes. She was so pretty, Jackson could barely concentrate, and promptly fell over a shelving cart, dumping books everywhere. However, he soon discerned that Ms. Holiday was *not* the reason the herd hung out in the library. The boys in the herd paid little attention to her or her dazzling smile, and the girls, even less. They actually read the books!

When the bell rang at the end of free period, the herd filed out into the hall. Jackson looked at the books they left behind. Duncan was reading a book on the chemical compounds in glue. Heathcliff's book was on military mind-control experiments. Matilda had been studying the aerodynamic qualities of rockets. Ruby was reading a guide to surviving hay fever, and Flinch, well, Jackson couldn't tell what he had been reading since the pages were covered in chocolate and nougat.

The nerd herd's reading material was as mysterious as they were. Hoping for better clues, Jackson decided to follow them home. At the end of the day he raced outside to wait for his targets, but they never came out! The other kids fled the school like pigs at a barbecue, but the herd was not among them. Maybe they were at band practice or a meeting of the *Star Trek* Fan Society, Jackson guessed, but when it grew dark, he had to accept that they had left without him noticing. As he trudged home in frustration, dodging the dozens of magnetized hubcaps his headgear attracted off of passing cars, he wondered if the herd actually lived in the school. He shook off the idea as silly, but there was certainly something odd about those kids.

After a week without learning much, Jackson caught a lucky break in class. His teacher, Mr. Pfeiffer, was famous for his lesson plans. Instead of earth science or say, grammar, Pfeiffer concentrated on a subject he was well acquainted with—himself. This particular day was no different. While Pfeiffer waxed on about his favorite vacations, Jackson watched the herd. And something extraordinary happened: All five of them sneezed at the same time. At first Jackson didn't think much of it. After all, nerds were always sneezing. But the sneeze was followed by something peculiar. No sooner had these nerds wiped their noses than bucktoothed Heathcliff marched to the front of the class and said something to Mr. Pfeiffer in a low voice. The teacher seemed almost mesmerized. He nodded enthusiastically, then gave Heathcliff a hall pass. All five of the nerds walked out of class. A moment later, Pfeiffer was back to discussing the benefits of cocoa butter and aloe vera.

If the simultaneous sneeze had happened once, Jackson wouldn't have given it a second thought, but several days later, during Pfeiffer's lecture on how he planned to redecorate his apartment, the herd went into another sneezing fit. As before, Heathcliff approached the teacher and whispered something, and a moment later the herd was dashing into the hall. Jackson realized he was witnessing a pattern and, also, that Pfeiffer was unqualified to educate children. The next time it happened, Jackson would be prepared.

A few days later, when the herd's sinus sirens wailed once

more, and when Pfeiffer gave the gang the go-ahead to leave, Jackson darted out into the hall after them. He looked one way and then the other, and spotted them as they raced around a corner.

"Hey! Wait!" he shouted. He wanted answers.

Flinch turned and spotted him, but quickly ran off after his friends. When Jackson rounded the corner, the hall was empty. Duncan, Ruby, Matilda, Heathcliff, and Flinch had vanished! Their only possible exit was a door at the end of the hall, but when Jackson opened it, he found a broom closet filled with mops and urinal cakes. Where had the herd gone?

"Son, are you lost?" a voice called to him from the other end of the hallway. Jackson turned and spotted the school's new janitor approaching. Jackson couldn't remember his name, but his appearance was unforgettable. He looked like a male model with broad shoulders and rugged blue eyes. He had a pronounced limp in his right leg, and he used his mop and bucket to help him get along. Still, he seemed dignified and intelligent. Jackson had heard some of the female teachers mooning over him and commenting on what an improvement he was over the old janitor, Mr. Pecko, who was short, had a lazy eye, and suffered from persistent mouth funk.

"No, sir. I just—" Jackson stammered.

The janitor was about to say something, but he was interrupted by a bellowing voice.

"Mr. Jackson Jones, aren't you supposed to be in class?" Charging toward Jackson and the janitor was Principal Dehaven, a little man with a curly perm and a moustache. He had stubby arms and legs, and a chest like a pickle barrel.

"I, um . . . ," Jackson said, realizing that telling the truth about spying on a bunch of nerds would make him sound like he'd been standing too close to the dry-erase markers.

"'Um,' is not an answer, young man," Dehaven growled. "The answer is 'Class, sir!' I'm not sure if you are aware of this, young man, but you are in a school. Perhaps you've heard that word before? 'School'?"

"Actually, sir," the janitor interjected, "Jackson was just asking me about a career as a janitorial engineer. I asked permission from his teacher to show him the ropes—you know, mopping, sweeping, scraping gum off the bottom of desks. He's showing a lot of promise, if you ask me, and I thought I'd give him a leg up on the competition."

"Is this true?" Dehaven eyeballed Jackson like he could see through him. "You want to be a janitor?"

Jackson looked to the janitor, then nodded. "It's my dream."

The principal nodded. "Well, I suppose that's all right. Though I must say, I think you're setting your sights a little high, Mr. Jones. Very well, then. Get on with it, Mr. . . . What is it, again?"

"Brand," the janitor said. "And I fully intend to, sir."

Dehaven turned and charged back down the hall leaving Jackson and Mr. Brand alone.

"Perhaps you should get back to class, Jackson," Mr. Brand said.

Jackson nodded and headed back down the hall.

"And Mr. Jones?" Brand called out just before Jackson turned the corner. "Don't forget what killed the cat."

That night, Jackson couldn't help but replay the scene in his head. He was sure the herd had gone down that hallway. How had Ruby, Heathcliff, Duncan, Matilda, and Flinch disappeared? A funny thought occurred to him. Could they have been hiding in the lockers that lined the hallway? He knew the nerd herd had probably been shoved into a few in their day, but would they lock themselves in them on purpose? And if they had, why?

He tossed and turned, feeling that odd tingling in the back of his head. Jackson was swimming through a secret and soon he would be able to see through it all the way to the bottom.

Jackson didn't have to wait long. The very next day, during Pfeiffer's lecture on his favorite television sitcoms, the nerds' noses went off again. Up from their seats they jumped and were out the door in a flash. Ignoring Dehaven's threats and the odd janitor's warning, Jackson raced right behind them. This time, however, he was careful not to be seen or heard. His stealth paid off. It was just as he had suspected! The nerds each climbed inside an unused locker and closed the doors behind them.

What a bunch of weirdos! Jackson thought. He opened the locker he had seen Duncan enter, his mind brimming with questions, but to his utter amazement, the locker was empty. He rushed over to the locker he had seen Ruby enter, but found only a couple of school books and a half-eaten orange. He rushed to Heathcliff's locker—empty. Then Matilda's—empty. Flinch's—empty, empty, empty! Where had they gone?

He was sure he was losing his mind. All that metal in his mouth must have seeped into his brain. He turned to head straight to the school nurse when he heard someone approaching from down the hallway. The rapid steps and heavy breathing told Jackson that Principal Dehaven was on his way. If the principal found him in the hallway again without a pass, he'd spend the rest of his natural life in detention. In desperation, he did the only thing he could think of to save himself. He climbed into a locker and closed the door.

Oh, the irony. How many nerds had he shoved into lockers?

He wasn't even sure numbers went up that high! And now, here he was, crammed into one himself.

"Where is that janitor?" he heard Dehaven grumble to himself as he stopped just outside Jackson's locker. "He's never around when I need him."

Jackson watched through the vents in the locker door. Dehaven was tapping his foot impatiently. Then he peered around, making sure he was alone, and did something terrible. He picked his nose.

"Gross," Jackson said.

Mr. Dehaven spun toward the locker. He stepped up close and peered into the vent, then tried the handle. Jackson gripped the edge of the metal door, preventing it from opening. After several moments, Dehaven gave up and stomped back the way he came.

Jackson realized he needed to get back to class before the principal returned, but when he tried to open the door, he found it was jammed. Jackson was trapped. He wanted to call out for help, but Dehaven would hear him. He worried that he might be stuck in the locker all day before someone discovered him. Heck, he might be in there for years! Explorers might open the locker eons in the future and discover him there, like some nerdy mummy in his gym-shoe-smelling sarcophagus.

"If you get me out of this, I swear I will always be good," he promised the heavens.

And then suddenly, a red light flashed above his head and the floor beneath him slid away. He couldn't see, and all he heard was his own screaming as he shot down a metal tube. Then there was an enormous roar, like someone had flipped on the world's largest ceiling fan, and a powerful wind came up from below. When Jackson looked down, he saw a huge wind turbine, blasting air at him and slowing his fall. Soon, he was hovering, like a loose feather, directly over the turbine's grate. A steel panel slid over the fan, and Jackson landed squarely on his feet. He hardly had time to thank his lucky stars before the floor tilted upward, revealing another hole. Jackson tumbled into it and rocketed along a twisty-turny slide. He went through a loop-de-loop, and just when he was sure he would barf, another hatch opened and he fell through it.

Much to his surprise he landed in an overstuffed chair. An oddly proper voice said, "Welcome to the Playground."

He was in a large square room as big as a baseball field. The floor was decorated in multicolored ceramic tiles, and the ceiling was held aloft by dozens of marble columns. Each wall was decorated with an elaborate mural dedicated to a different branch of science—biology, physics, geology, and chemistry. Scattered about the room were workstations. Some held computers, others elaborate experiments—vials of chemicals, half-built machines, water tanks. Mounted above all this were the largest television monitors Jackson had ever seen. They were broadcasting scenes from around the world: a man taking money from an ATM with the Eiffel Tower in the background, two men playing dominoes in Red Square, a woman and her son sightseeing at the Great Wall of China. Jackson realized these weren't television shows, but actual events caught by surveillance cameras around the globe. On several monitors, Jackson could see students from his school walking to class, sleeping at their desks, struggling to climb the rope in the gymnasium. It seemed every inch of Nathan Hale Elementary was under surveillance.

Tearing his attention away from the TVs, Jackson noticed a circular desk sitting on a platform at the center of the room. It was made from some kind of glass, inlaid with tiny computer circuits. Jackson walked over to take a closer look. When he touched the surface of the desk, a tiny blue orb floated out of a hole in the center. It spun like a tornado, then began to emit particles of light. The particles combined to form a three-dimensional picture of a snow-capped mountain range. It was so real, Jackson felt he could dip his hand into the snowmelt rushing down to the river below. He had never seen technology like it in his life. He wondered how the school could afford something this advanced when most of the students shared textbooks.

Suddenly, as if a bell had sounded somewhere, doors swung open around the room and dozens of people dressed in white lab coats and goggles rushed to the workstations. They didn't seem to notice Jackson.

He watched as a man climbed into a tank of water. He had a tiny green device in his nose and, once he was submerged, it was clear that the device was allowing him to breathe. In another corner of the room, a scientist wearing a bright orange jumpsuit that covered him from head to toe was handed a lit stick of dynamite. Jackson panicked, but when the dynamite exploded, the scientist appeared to be unharmed.

Jackson gaped in wonder as he moved about the room, examining one experiment after another, but his attention finally settled on a scientist working with a pink-nosed guinea pig. She plugged a computer cable into the back of a video monitor. The other end of the cable was inserted into the belly of the furry rodent. At once, the monitor came to life, broadcasting what appeared to be the guinea-pig's-eye view. A colleague came over to watch.

"I call it the 'guinea pig camera,'" the proud scientist announced to her colleague. "The team can give one of these to a suspect's child and it will record anything it sees or hears. Just plug in this cable and it downloads right onto your hard drive!"

The scientist continued her demonstration, aiming the furry animal in all directions. The image stopped on Jackson.

All at once, the scientists turned to face him. "How did you get in here?" one shouted.

"Uh, I'm lost," he said.

Before he could explain further, a siren went off and a voice announced: "We have an intruder in the Playground. Attention, all agents. We have an intruder in the Playground."

Jackson had no idea what was happening, but one thing was clear—he had not stumbled into the teacher's lounge.

END TRANSMISSION.

4

Each of the scientists the Hyena kidnapped and delivered to the secret lair at the North Pole went through the same process. Henchmen took their clothing and personal possessions and gave them orange prison jumpsuits. They were shoved into tiny cells without windows and told to sit tight until they were needed. They weren't allowed to use the phone, but they were well fed and even given magazines and books to help them pass the time. At last they were ushered into a large room filled with chalkboards and chairs. Half the chalkboards held a long, intricate equation. *X*s and *Y*s swam through it, and quite a number of question marks. The henchmen forced chalk into the scientists' hands and instructed them to fill in the missing numbers and finish the equation. They worked day and night, though it was clear none of them was sure exactly what the equation was or what it might solve.

It was during those long afternoons that the Hyena started to see Dr. Jigsaw's diabolical nature. What kind of black-hearted soul forced a person to do math problems? She remembered the math teacher she had had in the third grade who insisted that someday she would need long division. Three years later she was still waiting. But Jigsaw's evil went far beyond any math teacher's, because of how he reacted to the scientists' progress. Every few hours he would emerge from behind a locked door in the back of the room and study the equation. Sometimes he would get very excited and praise his hostages, but more often he would get violently angry, snatch an eraser, and obliterate days of work right before their eyes. The first few times this happened, the scientists took it in stride, but by the tenth time they were in tears.

The Hyena couldn't help but feel sympathy for the scientists. They all looked distraught and exhausted. But her sympathy quickly turned to anger. She wasn't supposed to have compassion! She was a professional assassin. She was supposed to have veins clogged with ice and a heart as black as coal. Contract killers didn't sit around worrying about their victims. She had to get herself under control. Sympathy was very unprofessional.

Eventually, one of the braver scientists stepped forward. "Dr. Jigsaw, this would be easier if you would tell us what this equation is meant to solve."

Jigsaw rolled back on his heels. "It's not obvious?"

The scientists shook their heads.

Jigsaw let out an exasperated sigh, grabbed a stick of chalk, and drew a picture of the Earth. At the top he drew a massive satellite dish and on each of the major continents he drew arrows pointing toward the other continents. The Hyena had no idea what any of it meant, but once Jigsaw's drawing was complete, the kidnapped scientists let out a collective gasp.

"You can't be serious!"

"You've lost your mind, Jigsaw!"

"It will never work!"

"It will never work?" Jigsaw cried as he spun around and walked back to his private room. "Follow me."

The henchmen shoved the scientists along and into Jigsaw's secret room. Eager to see what was inside, the Hyena followed the crowd. She was flabbergasted by what she found. The room was as big as a football field, with walls that rose to the clouds. There was no ceiling and it was bitterly cold. Dozens of henchmen dressed in heavy coats, gloves, and goggles rushed about working on a massive satellite dish pointed toward the sky.

"It has to work, my friends," Jigsaw said as he gestured to the dish. "You see, I've already built it."

5

Jackson's brain screamed for him to run, but when he spun around to flee, a metal slab dropped from the ceiling, blocking the exit. He saw other exits being cut off around the room. He raced toward the only open doorway he saw, but the scientists lined up to block his path. However, they were no match for the Fighting Tigers' former star quarterback! Jackson rushed forward, executing a block that knocked a scientist to the floor, and a stiff arm that kept another at bay. He weaved and danced around a couple of tables, and slipped through the open doorway just as a steel slab fell behind him.

When Jackson caught his breath, he found himself in another strange room, this one shaped like a circle with a mosaic of the universe laid into the floor. Aside from the shelves of dusty manuscripts that lined the walls, the only other thing in the room was a silver pedestal. The pedestal was covered in knobs, buttons, and blinking lights, and a large blue orb hovered above it, just like the one Jackson had seen in the other room. Hanging from the ceiling directly above the pedestal were more computer monitors and hundreds of thick, loose cables dangling like the arms of an electronic octopus. Jackson studied the pedestal and his heart soared. It was clearly some kind of computer, even if it did have more bells and whistles than most. It had to have e-mail too! He could send for help! He'd have the police, the FBI, the army, and the local Girl Scout troop kicking down the door of this screwy secret lab in no time.

Unfortunately, Jackson had no idea where to start. There was no mouse and no obvious power button. In desperation, he went to work pushing all the buttons, not sure of what they might do.

Then the strange voice he had heard after falling through the locker returned. "You have accessed the physical enhancement protocol of the National Espionage, Rescue, and Defense Society. Prepare for upgrade. Code name, please?"

"Are you talking to me?" Jackson asked, looking around.

"Yes. Have you chosen a code name?"

"I don't know what you're talking about," Jackson said. "I'm just trying to find a way out of this—"

The voice interrupted him. "No code name submitted.

Subject has twenty-four hours to log in a code name or an appropriate one will be assigned. Scanning for weaknesses."

Suddenly, the bookshelves on either side of Jackson moved away from the walls, revealing banks of little green lights. Each emitted lasers, which whisked across his body in odd patterns. They didn't cause him any pain, but they did make him nervous.

"Physical attributes are above normal range," the voice said. "Continuing to scan for weaknesses."

As the lasers continued to sweep across his body, there was an awesome bang on the door and a huge dent appeared, as if a giant had tossed a rhino against the steel. The scientists on the other side were trying to break down the door.

"Where's the e-mail program?" Jackson cried as he frantically pushed more buttons.

A bank of little red lights appeared on the pedestal. The machine began to beep and twitter and the orb above it began to spin. It turned slowly at first, but then whirled so fast it dazzled Jackson's eyes. A million light particles scattered around the room.

Crunch! A bigger dent appeared in the door.

The particles swirled over the walls and floor, eventually collecting into one unified shape—a three-dimensional skeleton floating directly before Jackson. It seemed to move as Jackson did. When he turned his head, it turned its head. When he raised his arm, it did the same. He reached toward the skeleton, but when his hands broke the image's surface, the figure disappeared. "It's a hologram," he said aloud.

When he pulled his arm away, the skeleton reappeared, this time showing a heart, lungs, kidneys, liver, and stomach. After that, a layer of muscles and veins was added to the skeleton.

"Internal organs within normal range. No chemical imbalances detected. No allergies detected. Scanning continues," the odd voice said.

Crunch! One of the door's bolted hinges bent and the screws that held it fell to the floor.

Now the skeleton was covered in skin. Eyeballs appeared, followed by hair and fingernails. Now it was clear to Jackson that the hologram was a three-dimensional portrait of him from the inside out. He only wished the computer would add some clothing.

The strange voice returned. "Weakness detected. Subject has extensive dental devices. Upgrade will take place in three . . ."

"Wait! What's an upgrade?"

"Two . . ."

Jackson started pushing buttons in a panic. "How do you stop this thing?"

"One. Upgrade commencing."

Suddenly, a leather chair rose out of the floor. Jackson fell into it, and before he could scramble out, his hands and feet were strapped down. The chair tilted back, then stretched out into a cot. Two spiderlike machines emerged from the jungle of cables above and lowered to just inches above Jackson's face. Each had eight arms, with different devices attached to the ends: knives, drills, and saw blades, all whirling and spinning wildly. Jackson opened his mouth to scream, only to have one of the arms use rubber hooks to pull back his lips from his teeth.

"Help!" he shouted, and though the pounding at the door continued, the scientists had yet to break through. Oh how Jackson wished he had been captured by them instead of the ruthless, faceless computer!

"Think pleasant thoughts," the voice said.

And then, everything went black.

6

For a professional killer with ice in her veins, the Hyena was pretty cute. She had platinum blonde hair and bright green eyes, long eyelashes, and a nose like a button. When she was seven years old, her mother decided to capitalize on her daughter's stunning good looks. She packed up their belongings, bought a used Winnebago, and plunged her daughter into the world of professional child beauty pageants. She dressed the Hyena in sparkly gowns, false eyelashes, and high-heeled shoes. Twice weekly she sent the little girl for spray-on tans that left her looking like a walking tangerine. She enrolled the Hyena in hip-hop, jazz, and modern dance classes. She sent her for voice, acting, and piano lessons twice a week. She hired coaches who taught the Hyena how to bat her eyes and flash a smile at the judges as she sang "Minnie the Moocher."

Their hard work paid off. The Hyena won hundreds of

trophies, received thousands of dollars in college scholarships, and had a collection of crowns to rival a princess's. She was named the Georgia Beef Beauty, Little Miss Florida Citrus, California's Canola Oil Charmer, Wisconsin Wheat Fairy, Dairy Princess of Lawrence, Kansas, and Idaho Spud Queen all in the same month. She was a bright, over-tanned representative of all six major food groups!

But it wasn't her good looks and spunky personality that won her so many competitions. What put her over the top every time was the talent portion. While some girls played the violin or

recited *Hamlet*, the Hyena gave an instructional lesson on how to fend off an attacker with flaming nunchakus. She slashed, jabbed, and dismembered a training dummy with a twinkle in her eye. The judges were impressed by her mercilessness. Or perhaps they voted for her out of fear. Regardless, the act was a smash.

Ever the show-woman, the Hyena's mother eagerly expanded the act to include more weapons: sai, daggers, and swords; billy clubs, Tasers, and brass knuckles. Their Winnebago was a rolling arsenal. The Hyena's mother also enrolled her daughter in whatever martial arts classes they could find as they journeyed across America. The Hyena learned judo in Juneau, aikido in Akron, jiujitsu in Jamestown, tae kwon do in Tallahassee, sambo in San Diego, kendo in Kansas City, Jogo do Pau in Jersey City, and kung fu in Kissimmee. As a backup, she learned tap dancing in Tulsa. Unfortunately, her mom's enthusiasm backfired when the Hyena announced she wanted to do something else with her life—something more dignified than prancing around in a cocktail dress.

She wanted to become a professional assassin.

Sadly, as the Hyena had discovered, the life of a freelance professional contract killer was not all that it was cracked up to be. In fact, she hadn't actually gotten to kill anyone yet. And because of her lack of experience, she was forced to accept less desirable jobs in the world of professional crime—namely, being a goon. Not a highly trained killer! Not even a minion or a henchman. A goon! If the other contract killers found out she was kidnapping people, she would be a laughingstock.

Now, the average person might not know the difference between an assassin and a minion, a henchman and a goon, but they are as different as apples and oranges. Assassins, naturally, assassinate people and are paid incredible sums of money to do it. They wear a lot of black and sometimes have really cool scars on their faces. And they have nicknames like the Scorpion, or Le Tigre, or Black Widow.

The next step down is a minion. In a nutshell, a minion's job is to fulfill the often impossible demands of his evil boss. If the boss says he wants an army of man-eating gophers, a minion has to get on the phone and track down some of the furry little demons. If the boss says he wants a secret lair on the moon, the minion has to order the supplies of Tang and freeze-dried space ice cream that will be needed in the rocket. Other major responsibilities include praising the boss's evil plots and feeding his psychotic pet (typically a venomous snake or a tarantula or a horribly mutated house cat). Basically, a minion is a personal assistant—only an evil personal assistant. It's not as cool as being an assassin, but you get health and dental insurance, and the boss usually pays into your 401(k).

After minions, there's henchmen. Henchmen are grunts who do all the hard labor. They build the secret fortress and massive doomsday devices. They usually guard the lair and, in a pinch, can be called in to help push the boss's enemies into the shark tank. All in all, the work is fine. It's the uniform that stinks. See, henchmen have to wear ridiculous costumes. If your boss is a lunatic obsessed with bears, you can be sure you're wearing a big furry suit to work. If your boss dresses like the ringleader of a circus, you better buy yourself a pair of stilts or some clown shoes. It's downright humiliating, and, unfortunately, workers in the crime industry do not have strong union representation.

Goons, however, are at the very bottom of the villain food chain. Most are no more than muscle for mad scientists, corrupt politicians, evil geniuses, and megalomaniacs. They kidnap people, break a lot of legs, and make a lot of threats (all while cracking their knuckles for dramatic effect). Most of them are misshapen, with huge jaws, arms like gorillas, and heads resembling damaged pumpkins. The Hyena did not want to be a goon. Sure, it beat competing in the Putnam County Pancake Pageant, but it would still look terrible on her résumé. It was very easy to get typecast in her business, and once you got pegged as a goon, it was hard to work your way up.

But a paycheck is a paycheck. The Hyena needed the money, so she was doing her best to put her concerns aside and follow a few simple rules: (1) Don't date the other goons. (2) Get the money up front and in cash (it was tempting to work for free, especially when your boss promised to give you a small continent or chain of islands to rule when he was in charge of the world, but promises don't pay the bills). And (3) Don't criticize the boss.

Rule number three was giving the Hyena trouble. Dr. Jigsaw was perfectly pleasant to her. She rarely saw him (which was good because the bizarre perfection of his surgically designed face unnerved her), and he brought in donuts every Friday for the staff. But though he provided a happy work environment, he neglected important details. For instance, he had failed to tell her that some of the scientists on her kidnapping list were world-class athletes. Dr. Hammond was a semiprofessional boxer. Dr. Beldean had once been a Navy SEAL. Professor Church was incredibly fast with a slide rule. A little information could have spared the Hyena a lot of grief and quite a few bruises. When she asked Jigsaw if he was aware that Dr. Banyon had once been a pro wrestler, he nodded and offered her the last jelly donut.

So when the Hyena went after her next target—a Professor Joseph Lunich, who was the world's preeminent expert on magnetism—she wondered what she didn't know about him. Jigsaw was obsessed with Lunich's latest invention—the miniature tractor beam—and not only wanted the Hyena to bag him, but his machine as well. Jigsaw claimed the device was revolutionary and essential to his plans. The Hyena couldn't have cared less about some goofy machine. She was more concerned about whether Lunich had been an Ultimate Fighter or a defensive tackle before he invented it.

The professor's lab was in an empty warehouse on the campus of Vassar College in Poughkeepsie, New York. The Hyena slinked inside and found a good hiding space to wait for the scientist. He arrived hours later and went right to work on his device. The Hyena quickly understood why Jigsaw found the miniature tractor beam so intriguing.

Lunich stuffed a tiny pointed device into a potted plant, pushed a button on the device's side, and aimed the beam that shot out of it at a pickup truck parked inside the warehouse space. Then he climbed into the pickup truck, started the engine, and floored the gas. The truck's powerful engine throbbed as its wheels spun in vain. The tractor beam bathed it in a green energy and held it fast. The truck couldn't move an inch; it was held in place by a device no bigger than a pencil. Then, remarkably, the truck began to slide backward—it was being pulled across the room by the tiny device.

When the experiment was over, the Hyena stepped out of her hiding place. "I have to admit, I think your machine is pretty awesome," she said to the startled scientist. "So does my boss. He'd like you to show him how it works. So, how about it? Want to give a kid a break and go quietly?"

Unfortunately, the only break Dr. Lunich gave was for the door. In a flash, he was gone, leaving the would-be assassin dumfounded. The Hyena would later learn that Dr. Jigsaw had neglected to tell her that the professor was not only a brilliant scientist, but also a record-breaking sprinter.

What happened next was an exercise in humiliation. Lunich raced across the campus as gracefully as a deer. He weaved through the maze of paths, shouting for help along the way. The Hyena was sure the campus police or some Good Samaritan would arrive at any moment. Worse, she realized, she was never going to be able to catch the doctor in her high-heeled boots. When she fell in the grass for the fifth time, she noticed she had broken a heel. Disgusted, she vowed to track down and kill the people who designed women's shoes. In her frustration, she pulled the boot off and angrily tossed it in Lunich's direction. To her utter amazement, it sailed across the lawn and smacked the doctor squarely in the back of the head. He crumpled to the ground and lay still.

It was a lucky break for shoe designers everywhere.

END TRANSMISSION.

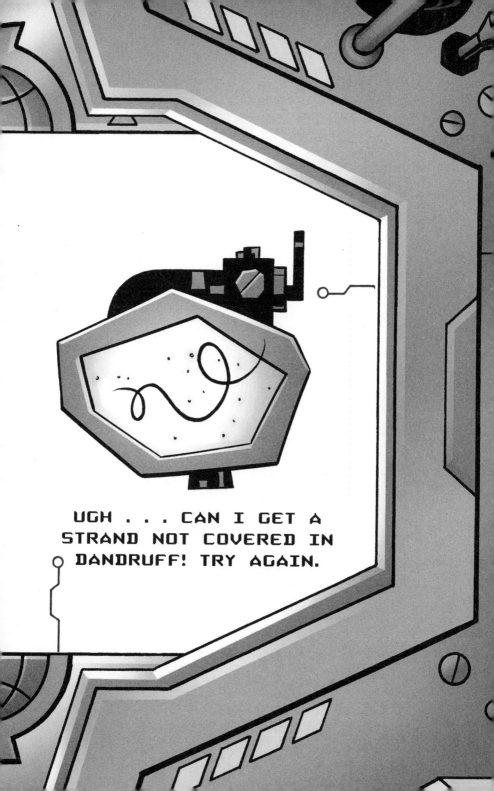

7

As Jackson hovered between consciousness and oblivion, he could make out several dark figures standing over him. They spoke angrily to one another.

"How did he find his way down here?"

"He's been watching us."

"Well, I guess we have to wipe his mind."

"My pleasure."

"We can't wipe his mind. Benjamin gave him the upgrades. We can't set him loose with all that technology. He's got about ten billion dollars worth of nanobytes in his mouth. We should call for the director."

"Since when do we listen to the director? I'm team leader and I say he needs a mind wipe."

Jackson sat up groggily. He wished someone would turn on the light so he could see who was talking about him. "Where am I?"

"What did he say?"

"Who knows? He's got so much metal in his mouth."

"Who are you people?" Jackson said.

"He sounds like a baby. Do you want a bottle, baby?"

"Don't tease him."

"As if he deserves better. Hold his arms."

"I got him," another said as two very strong hands clamped down on Jackson's shoulders.

Suddenly, a shaft of light illuminated two of the biggest front teeth Jackson had ever seen on a person. Jackson had seen donkeys with smaller teeth. Looking at them caused a strange sensation to come over Jackson. His head felt like it was full of soup and his thoughts seemed heavy. He wanted to leap from the chair but he'd lost the will to do so.

"Just stare into my teeth," a voice said.

And then all the lights came on, and the owners of the voices were revealed. The hands holding Jackson belonged to tiny Flinch Escala and the giant teeth that threatened to steal his soul were attached to Heathcliff Hodges. Ruby Peet, Duncan Dewey, and Matilda Choi were standing nearby. Behind them was another figure, a tall, broad-shouldered man carrying a mop. He had just walked in and he was angry. It was the school janitor, Mr. Brand.

"What is going on in here?" he demanded.

"Look! You gotta help me," Jackson said, "'cause these nerds are holding me against my will—"

Ruby interrupted him. "He's seen the Playground. He's gotten the upgrades. We have to wipe his mind."

Mr. Brand hobbled forward, using his mop as support. He stood over Jackson and peered at him closely.

"There's a very good chance that his brain can't take it, Pufferfish," Mr. Brand said. "I don't want another Stevie Lazar on our hands."

Jackson knew Stevie Lazar. Not long ago he had been a national spelling bee champion and on his way to NASA's space camp for a week during fall break. Then, suddenly, he lost interest in school, friends, and bathing. Now he spent his days picking his nose, drooling, and singing nursery rhymes to a filthy sock puppet he carried with him everywhere he went. He had become a moron overnight. Were these kids responsible? Had they turned an honor roll student into a kid who stuffed his pockets with frozen fish sticks?

"How did this happen?" Brand continued.

"He found his way into the Playground and the science team chased him in here. Somehow he accessed the upgrade program," Duncan said. "It must have been blind luck."

"Or maybe he's a spy," Ruby said.

"I doubt very much that he's a spy, Pufferfish," Brand said. "Any suggestions other than erasing his brain?"

"Lock him up in a cell and throw away the key," Matilda said.

Heathcliff agreed. "Remember how he treated us—spitwads, swirlies, atomic wedgies. He's a menace. Lock him up, wipe his mind—either way, we're doing the world a favor."

Flinch shook his fist enthusiastically. With the lights on, Jackson could see the scrawny boy was wearing a strange harness that covered his arms and legs. A pulsing light flashed on a plate on his chest, right beneath a large knob. "Or you could let me throw him in the ocean. I'm strong like bull!"

Jackson was startled by the herd's anger. He'd never heard anyone talk about him with such venom. Everyone liked him. Sure, he'd had a setback lately in the popularity department, but everyone knew he was a great guy.

"People, just calm down," Brand said as he went to work unfastening the straps that tied Jackson to the bed. "There's not going to be any mind wiping or throwing anyone in the ocean."

"You're not saying we're going to kill him, are you?" Matilda asked. She broke into excited gasps, then used her inhaler to calm herself.

Brand shook his head and helped Jackson to his feet. "Hardly. I'm letting him go."

Ruby clenched her fists. "Mr. Brand, as team leader I believe that's my decision, and I say we lock him up."

"Pufferfish, let me make this clear one more time. I'm the boss and this kid is going home," Mr. Brand said.

Brand pushed a button on the wall and a glass tube came down from above and encased Jackson. He was sucked upward, and a moment later he was tumbling out of the lockers and onto the cold floor.

Jackson wanted to tell his family what he had experienced but was afraid they would think he had lost his mind. Not that he would blame them. He couldn't expect his father and brother to believe that his elementary school was the headquarters of a secret organization run by five nerds and a janitor with a bad leg. Who would believe that? He wasn't sure he believed it.

Maybe he had imagined the whole thing. Maybe he was sick. The tater tots at lunch *had* smelled a little funky.

Still, he felt he should say something. He waited until dinnertime.

"Dad, something happened at school today," he said.

His brother, Chaz, who was fully dressed for football practice, laughed. "Did someone steal your lunch money again?"

Jackson's dad wasn't listening. He was busy spoon-feeding his closest friend and constant companion in life, a pit bull named Butch. Butch was a fat, sour animal who was bitterly jealous of Jackson and Chaz. He growled and snapped whenever the boys

were around, but their father was convinced the animal farted rainbows. Butch's worst quality, however, was his ability to steal their father's attention.

"Dad, I really need to tell you something. It's important," Jackson said.

Mr. Jones set down the spoon, causing Butch to erupt in fury. "OK, Jackson. You have my attention. Did you get bullied again?"

"I'm—that's not what I want to tell you," Jackson stammered.

The telephone rang in the kitchen.

"Can you hold on for a sec?" his father said as he got up and headed for the kitchen. "Feed Butch while I'm gone."

The boys exchanged pained expressions.

"Well, I got practice," Chaz said, shoveling a heaping bite of Swiss steak into his mouth and then getting up from the table.

"Jerk," Jackson called after him.

"I'll pray for you, Nerdatron," Chaz said, and disappeared out the front door, leaving Jackson and Butch alone.

The pit bull eyed the boy with contempt.

"Right back at you, ugly," Jackson said.

Butch exploded with angry snarls, causing Mr. Jones to pop his head into the room. "What's going on?"

"Nothing," Jackson said, and his father disappeared again. "Only your dog is insane," Jackson muttered.

Jackson took a seat near the dog and picked up the big wooden spoon his father used to feed the beast. He loaded it with veal, but, unfortunately, as soon his hand got close, the evil canine lunged for it and nipped him hard. Jackson clenched his teeth and tried again. This time the dog nearly took a chunk of his thumb.

"If you do that one more time, I'm going to let you starve," Jackson threatened.

When the third spoonful approached, Butch sunk his teeth into the side of Jackson's hand. Jackson was about to cry out when he felt an odd swirling in his mouth. It felt as if his braces had come to life. They were moving left and right and up and down, and then his mouth flew open and two long metallic tentacles shot out. One snatched Butch by the jaws and forced them open, while the second grabbed the plate with the veal and poured it all into the dog's mouth. When every last chunk was inside, the tentacles forced the dog to chew.

"That was your principal," Jackson's dad said as he came back into the room.

Jackson looked down and saw that the odd appendages had slipped back into his mouth. Butch looked stunned.

"He says you've been cutting classes and disappearing," Mr. Jones said as he sat back down at the table.

"That's what I wanted to tell you about—"

Jackson's father shook his head. "Son, four weeks ago you

were the most popular kid in school. Now you've been cut from the football team, your grades are in the toilet, and you're turning into a delinquent. What is going on with you?"

Jackson was about to explain, but his father stopped him, again.

"Look at your brother. Chaz is an all-star. He's dependable. He's starting at quarterback as a freshman in high school. He's well liked and has a million friends. If you want to know what I expect from you, just take a look at him."

Jackson's face reddened with anger and embarrassment.

"Whatever is causing this turnaround in you is a bad influence. Get rid of it, Jackson. Get your act together."

Jackson's dad turned to Butch. "You want to go for a walk, big guy?"

The dog raced out of the room.

"What's got into him?" Mr. Jones asked.

Jackson watched his dad leave the room. After a moment, he shook off his hurt and hurried out to the garage to search in his father's old toolbox for a pair of pliers. When he found them, he ran back inside, climbing the stairs two at a time until he reached the bathroom, and closed the door tight behind him. He flipped on the light and stepped in front of the mirror. He opened his mouth to study his braces. They were moving! He could see them swarming here and there like worker ants. What had the nerds called them? Nanobytes? Regular braces were bad enough. The last thing he needed were braces made from tiny supercomputers.

He had to get rid of them. But as soon as he put the pliers in his mouth, his braces lashed out like a whip and knocked the tool out of his hand. On the next try, they snatched the pliers out of his hand and smacked him on the top of his head with them.

Jackson gave up. He went to his room and threw himself on the bed. He knew he was in big trouble. Whatever that strange computer had done to him, it had made him dangerous. He wondered how long it would be before his braces hurt someone. He imagined himself being tried and sentenced to life in prison for assault with a deadly dental device. He wondered what life would be like for a fifth grader in a federal penitentiary. Eventually he fell asleep and dreamed of a life on a chain gang, fixing the roads as Principal Dehaven stood over him shouting his name, over and over again.

When he woke, it was still dark out. He sat up, waited for his eyes to adjust, and then screamed and nearly fell out of bed.

Mr. Brand was sitting on the edge of his mattress. He looked completely different than he did at school. His face was shaved, his hair was washed, and he was dressed in an expensive-looking dark gray suit. In his hand he held a small black case.

"How did you get in my window?" Jackson cried. "I keep it locked."

Brand smiled. "It's a spy thing."

"Oh," Jackson said, climbing to his feet. "That's what you are—a spy?"

"Special Agent Alexander Brand," the man said, reaching out his hand. Jackson eyed him suspiciously and refused to take it. "I'm the director of NERDS."

"The director of what?"

Brand sighed. "The National Espionage, Rescue, and Defense Society. NERDS. It's an unfortunate acronym." He reached into his pocket and removed a small blue orb much like the two Jackson had seen at the Playground. The spy pushed a button on its side, and familiar blue particles swirled out of it. "I'm kind of new to the organization, so I thought I'd bring an expert. Say hello, Benjamin."

"Hello, Agent Brand," said the now familiar voice. "Your requested data is ready. Shall we begin?"

"Yes," Brand said.

"Very well. Welcome to an introduction to the National Espionage, Rescue, and Defense Society, also known as NERDS. Allow me to introduce myself."

Suddenly, the blue particles merged and a chubby old man in leggings and tiny spectacles appeared. He was balding, but wore his hair long in the back. Jackson recognized him at once. "You're Benjamin Franklin."

"Actually, Jackson, I'm the holographic representation of the teams' supercomputer technology. I have a level-four artificial intelligence and upon request can appear as America's great elder statesman, but the true Mr. Franklin has been dead for many years. However, you can call me Benjamin."

Jackson reached out to shake the figure's hand, but this only caused the image to ripple and smear.

Benjamin smiled. "Perhaps we should get started."

Suddenly, Jackson's room disappeared into a three-dimensional desert landscape so real he started to sweat. A beautiful pyramid rose up right before him, as well as thousands of dark-skinned men and women in tunics. They were gathered about listening to a single figure dressed in robes and a crown. Jackson guessed he was a king. He raised his hands to the sun above.

"Many people consider the real Benjamin Franklin to be America's first spy, but I am in no way the world's first. No, the secret agent has been around since the earliest days of recorded history. Akhenaten, the controversial Pharaoh of Egypt, enlisted his own son, Tutankhamun, to keep a careful eye on his enemies."

The hologram revealed a small boy wearing a crown and beautiful robes. He was huddling behind a column, listening to the conversation of two men who lurked in the shadows.

"Since then, spies have been used by countless leaders," Benjamin continued as the Egyptian setting vanished only to be replaced with three-dimensional portraits of various historical figures: Julius Caesar, Cleopatra, Napoleon Bonaparte, Attila the Hun, Richard the Lionheart, Queen Elizabeth, Abraham

Lincoln, Winston Churchill, and Fidel Castro. Suddenly, the images faded, leaving Benjamin alone.

"But secret agent work was dangerous. Spies were often killed in the line of duty. Then in the nineteen thirties and forties, everything changed. The first American computers became operational."

Benjamin disappeared, only to be replaced by the image of a massive computer that more than filled Jackson's room.

"It's as big as a house," Jackson said.

"The Mark 1, which became operational in 1944, was for the most part just a gigantic calculator, but it ushered in the age of technology, especially in the world of espionage. Soon agents could send information around the world in seconds. They could monitor targets from satellites, and they had high-tech gadgets at their disposal. But there were problems."

The Mark 1 disappeared, and in its place was a spy driving a sharp sports car along the Pacific Coast Highway. He wiped some sweat from his brow and eyed a panel of red buttons on his dash, with labels like "rocket launcher" and "turbo boost." The spy searched the buttons until he found one labeled "air conditioner." But when he tried to push it, he accidentally punched one that read "ejector seat" instead, and a moment later he was flying out of the top of the car and into the ocean.

"Most of the agents were not good with technology," Benjamin explained.

The road vanished and now Jackson saw a man in a tuxedo,

surrounded by ninjas. He pushed a button on his watch and a thin red laser fired, cutting the villains to ribbons. Proud of himself, the spy straightened his tie but forgot to turn off his watch, cutting off his own arm. His image was replaced by that of an agent removing a stick of gum from a package labeled "exploding gum." She popped it into her mouth and started to chew. Just watching her face, Jackson could tell the woman had accidentally swallowed the gum. A moment later her face vanished from view, but the explosion was deafening. Benjamin returned.

"It became clear that computers, technology, and science did not always mix with agents used to the field, and it was decided that a team of techno-savvy spies was needed, to take advantage of America's growing computer capabilities. A team of people perfectly comfortable with machines and gadgets."

The scene changed and Jackson found himself standing in the middle of an empty lot. Construction was underway on a seemingly normal building, but the lot was swarming with military police and the work was being done at night.

"There was only one group of people in the country with no fear of technology: children. The government quickly realized the advantages of recruiting children to do clandestine work. They are small, and adults often ignore them and underestimate their abilities and intelligence. In other words, children make great spies. So, in 1977, the government formed the National Espionage, Rescue, and Defense Society."

Jackson watched as the construction crew went into fast forward. Before his eyes, the empty lot became his school, Nathan Hale Elementary.

"Membership in the organization follows strict rules. Only a child can be an agent. Each agent is retired from active duty at the age of eighteen. No one can know of the NERDS' existence. Their work is done in secret."

The picture changed and Jackson saw the nerd herd, only each of them was doing amazing things.

"The current team consists of Duncan Dewey, code name Gluestick, a boy who can walk on walls and create powerful polymers by enhancing the glue he loves to eat."

Jackson watched Duncan's chubby little body leaping from wall to wall on the holographic projection. Duncan ran along one wall, then hung upside down from the ceiling. There was also video of him wiping his sticky skin on walls to seal cracks and bind doors. It was amazing, yet no sooner had he appeared than he was replaced by an image of Matilda.

"Matilda Choi, code name Wheezer, has always suffered from bronchial asthma, keeping her from athletic achievement and, occasionally, from walking around the block. But with the help of nano-powered inhalers, she can not only breathe freely, but fly as well. Her inhalers double as blowtorches to burn through steel doors, and as concussion blasts to knock down enemies."

Matilda soared into the air. The next image showed her

using the inhalers to burn a hole in the hull of a ship, and then to blast the crew as they ran to challenge her. She vanished and was replaced with Heathcliff.

"Heathcliff Hodges, code name Choppers, has an unfortunate set of buckteeth, but after a special nano-designed hallucinogenic whitening treatment, Hodges can use them to control the minds of people and many animals."

Heathcliff was shown hypnotizing a pack of wild dogs to chase down a villain. Then there was an image of him being backed into a corner by sword-wielding ninjas. He smiled and the ninjas dropped their swords and raised their hands in surrender. Heathcliff's face quickly morphed into Julio Escala's. Julio's tiny, shaky frame was quickly overlaid with the harness Jackson had seen him wearing.

"An important addition to the team is Julio Escala, code name Flinch. Flinch is intensely hyperactive, but now his busy body's nervous energy has been channeled into a special suit that converts it into superhuman strength and speed."

Jackson watched as Julio lifted a car off the ground like it was a newspaper, then saw him racing down a freeway, outrunning a BMW.

Running Julio became Ruby Peet, who scratched at her skin like an old dog with a bad case of the mange. A moment later, her body was swelling like a balloon.

"Ruby Peet, code name Pufferfish, has the most severe

case of allergies in documented history. She has extraordinary reactions to everything from peanuts to pizza, even swelling up when exposed to emotions like fear, anger, and love. What could be seen as a weakness has now been enhanced into an incredible ability. Her allergies warn her of danger and dishonesty in others. She is the team's current leader."

Benjamin continued. "Like their predecessors, the newest members of NERDS operate in shadows, using their weaknesses as strengths, monitoring the globe for possible conflicts, and fighting for the security of the world. Together, they are the world's last, best hope. When the best of the best can't get it done, NERDS can. Ta-ta for now."

The blue particles vanished, and Benjamin with them. Jackson found his bedroom returned to normal once more.

"Why are you telling me all of this?" Jackson said as he turned to Mr. Brand.

"Because I want you to join the team," the spy replied.

"Why me?"

Brand smiled. "I've just taken over as director, but I can already see the team has become too set in their ways, too isolated. A new perspective is just the thing they need to shake them up. You're a gifted athlete."

"True."

"And you're a born leader."

"It's like you know me."

"Plus, I've been watching you for some time, Jackson. You are a snoop. You spy on your friends and teachers and you're good at it. You managed to find your way into the Playground."

"So I'm very clever. That doesn't make me a spy," Jackson said.

"No, what makes you a spy is that tingling feeling you get when you are about to uncover a secret."

Jackson was stunned. How could Brand know about the tingling?

"I've been doing this work for a long time," Agent Brand continued. "I know when someone has what it takes. Plus, you have the incredible upgrade that Benjamin gave you."

"I can't be a spy," Jackson said. "Spies have to fly all over the world. What would I tell my dad?"

"Most of our missions take place during school hours. At other times, you can rely on this," the spy said as he reached down and picked up his black case. He opened the lid.

"A clarinet?"

"Tell your family you want to learn to play an instrument so you can join the marching band. Musical education takes a lot of time, especially after school. Your father will think you're just busy. He will never guess you are saving the world. And if he does, well, we always have Heathcliff's teeth. He can wipe his memory."

"What about school? He'll notice if my grades drop, and they are already dragging the ground."

"Jackson, we can't do your homework and take tests for you, but you'll have access to some of the finest minds in the world. You saw those scientists in the Playground. They'll tutor you."

Jackson was dumbfounded. He tried to imagine himself as a spy, but his mind was blank. "Can I think about it?" he said. "This is a big decision and I'm very much in demand these days. I really need to weigh my options."

Agent Brand nodded. "Of course. Think about it carefully, Jackson. We would pretty much own you until you're eighteen years old, but you would help keep millions, maybe even billions of people safe."

The spy reached into his pocket, pulled out a sealed envelope, and placed it in Jackson's hand. "When you're ready to serve your country, read this and follow the instructions."

Jackson glanced down at the envelope. "What is it?" But there was no answer. When he looked back up, the spy was gone.

In the world of professional crime there are four kinds of bosses: (1) Those who are obsessed with taking over the world in order to save it. They think they're actually heroes, ending one kind of world so that the survivors can pick up the pieces and start anew. (2) Those who want to destroy the world because of some perceived injustices from childhood or a time when colleagues laughed at their revolutionary ideas. Scientists are always laughing at each other, and it really irks some of them. (3) Those motivated by greed. For them, taking over the world is just another opportunity to drain it of all its money and resources. (4) The clinically insane type. The crazy bosses are prone to angry outbursts, paranoia, and unprovoked killing of underlings. They pore over their plans and doomsday devices, neglecting to shave or take a shower, and are baffled that those around them can't see the genius of their ideas.

The Hyena had begun to suspect that Dr. Felix Jigsaw was the fourth kind of boss. He rambled on and on to an imaginary colleague whom he was convinced was trying to sabotage his work. He ate nothing but bean sprouts, whole tea bags, and uncooked egg noodles, and he had a nasty habit of killing people when he didn't get his way. If it hadn't been for the guaranteed raise after ninety days, the Hyena would have quit.

But the killing and the unusual diet were only half of it. Every morning the Hyena and Dumb Vinci stood with the kidnapped scientists and watched Dr. Jigsaw do his daily workout routine. Jigsaw did one hundred one-armed push-ups. Fifty for his left arm and fifty for his right. When he was finished he would do one hundred lunges, one hundred shoulder presses, one hundred calf raises, and one hundred standing rows, fifty on each limb. It was a grueling workout, but what was even more painful was listening to Jigsaw's lecture on the importance of symmetry, how essential it was to be equally strong on both sides of the body.

One morning after his workout, Dumb Vinci brought Dr. Jigsaw the tiny pencil-shaped device the Hyena had found in Dr. Lunich's lab. Jigsaw studied it closely, turning it over and over, as if it were a beautiful flower.

"Dr. Lunich, tell me about your invention," Jigsaw said. The Hyena was surprised by the man's excitement. Jigsaw was nearly salivating.

Despite his kidnapping, Dr. Lunich had not lost his courage. He shook his head and turned up his nose.

"Dr. Lunich, that is bad manners. I invited you here to my lab. Don't you want to be friends?"

"I was not invited. I was kidnapped just like all the others," Lunich said, gesturing to the cowering men and women who stood behind him. "You should let us go before you get in more trouble."

Dr. Jigsaw sighed and turned to the Hyena. "Mindy, dear, sometimes I wonder if I have what it takes to be a scientist. You see, I hate setbacks. I know it's part of the job, and heaven knows I've had many. Some have been my fault—wrong turns I've made during my research, lack of imagination, exhaustion. But more often than not, my setbacks have been the result of working with lazy and small-minded people, bureaucrats, and pencil pushers. If I could only surround myself with passionate, open-minded thinkers, my plans would already have been completed. Take Iceland and Greenland—if I had the support of the scientific community, then they wouldn't have slammed into each other so hard and perhaps—"

"You did that? You moved Greenland? People were killed!" Lunich said.

"My point exactly, and you have no one else to blame but yourself. All I'm asking for is some help with some equations and a little insight on your remarkable device. Don't you want things to go better, Dr. Lunich?"

"You can forget it, Jigsaw!" Lunich shook his head. "I fear how you might use my invention."

"Then let me explain," the doctor said. "I have built a machine that can move continents from one place to the other with a blast of energy. Unfortunately, the machine is unable to move them precisely where I want them. Now, you've built an amazing machine, and I believe that if I can link my satellite to your tractor beam, I can literally tow everything where it's supposed to go."

"*Supposed* to go? I won't help you. In fact, *we're all* through with you." Lunich gestured to the other scientists. "You'll get no more help from us."

Jigsaw stomped his feet like a child whose mother has just refused him cookies.

"You don't have to be rude! If you don't want to be friends, that's fine with me!" Jigsaw shouted. He looked like he was about to storm off, but he hesitated for a moment. He stared at Lunich's face as if he were cataloging his features.

"Doctor, has anyone ever told you that your left ear is slightly bigger than your right ear?"

Lunich scowled impatiently. "No, no one has ever told me that."

"It's really disconcerting. Now that I notice it, I find it difficult to see the rest of your face. It's truly grotesque. I don't know how you live with yourself."

"You are clearly unwell," Lunich said with disgust.

"I just can't bear to look at it a second longer," Jigsaw said, then pushed a button on his wristwatch. The floor beneath Dr. Lunich slid open and he plummeted downward. A flash of fire and a puff of smoke rose from below, along with a terrible scream.

The Hyena thought her eyes might pop out of her head.

"Well, friends," Jigsaw said, waving the miniature tractor beam at the whimpering geniuses. "We're going to have to do this the old-fashioned way. Let's break it open and see how it works."

9

Jackson walked the hallways of Nathan Hale Elementary with a sense of wonder. The boring old cookie-cutter building he had never given a second thought to now seemed to be brimming with secrets. Every door might lead to a hidden room. Every face in the hall could belong to an international spy. He wondered if any of the other kids suspected anything. What would they think if they knew the world's very existence was owed to these hallways? Yet at the same time, Jackson had serious reservations about joining Brand's team. For one, he was worried he'd get killed, which was something he generally tried to avoid. And two, even with their souped-up technology, there were still nerds. All five of them were wheezing, whiny misfits.

Joining the group would mean giving up on ever being popular again. Even though his former friends had shunned him, Jackson still had hopes that they would give him another chance. If he accepted Brand's invitation, he could flush all his dreams down the toilet.

The more he thought about it, the more he realized that becoming a nerd, albeit a nerd who was also a secret agent, was not for him. No, he'd keep doing what he was doing and eventually he'd find his rightful place in the spotlight again. After all, once his old friends got a look at what he could do with his superbraces, he'd be the most popular kid in school. He reached into his pocket and felt the envelope that the spy had given him and knew what had to be done. He shoved the boys' bathroom door open and stepped inside.

"Thanks, but no thanks," he said as he crunched the envelope into a ball and tossed it into the toilet bowl. He was leaning over to flush it down when he heard the bathroom door open. He turned to see who it was and saw a group of his former friends, led by Brett. They were laughing and slugging one another in the arm, a game they seemed to play all the time. Instinctively, Jackson smiled at them. After all, they had been best friends for years. But when Brett sneered at him, he knew he had made a mistake.

"Hey, Braceface," Brett said. "How many toothbrushes do you go through in a day?"

The other boys exploded into obnoxious giggles.

Jackson felt his face flush. Before he could think, a nasty

reply escaped his lips, "Hey Brett, you still using those big-boy diapers at bedtime?"

Brett's face fell. His nightly bedwetting was a secret the two boys had shared since the second grade, when Jackson had spent the night at Brett's house and they had gone hog-wild over pizza, candy, and root beer after root beer. Jackson had woken several times in the night to visit the bathroom. Brett had slept like a rock—a rock floating on a soggy mattress. The next morning, in front of Jackson, Brett's mom had informed her son that from now on he would have to wear "pull-up pants," which everyone knew was code for diapers. Horrified, Brett swore Jackson to secrecy.

Jackson felt bad about revealing the secret and began to make an earnest apology, when Brett grabbed him by the collar and forced him back inside the bathroom stall. Then, with the help of the other boys, he shoved Jackson headfirst into the toilet bowl. Someone flushed and the water swirled around Jackson's ears. He was drowning, but there were too many hands holding him down. He kicked and punched and finally freed himself. Gagging and spitting, he managed to turn his head toward his attackers. They shrank back in terror. His braces! They had transformed into four metallic lobster claws, snapping and lunging at the bullies.

"Freak!" Brett shouted, scrambling for the bathroom door.

"No!" Jackson cried. "Wait. They're really cool."

His friends rushed out of the bathroom, leaving him alone on the floor. He lay there for a long time, fighting back tears. It was clear that his former life was officially over. As he got to his feet, he found a soggy wad of paper crumpled beneath him. It was the envelope. He scooped it up and opened it gingerly. Inside was a blurry handwritten note.

Go to the cafeteria. Ask the lunch lady for the creamed corn. Welcome to the National Espionage, Rescue, and Defense Society.

Jackson reread the words over and over to make sure he understood them. What did creamed corn have to do with becoming a spy?

He hurried down the hallway, leaving soggy footprints behind him.

The fifth grade was halfway through their lunch break, so the line in the cafeteria was short. Jackson hopped onto the end and soon stepped up to the counter. There he found the lunch lady chewing on an extinguished cigar. Jackson had never noticed her husky forearms before or, for that matter, how hairy they were. He had never noticed her five o'clock shadow before, either.

"What'll you have, kid?" the lunch lady asked in a rather deep voice.

"I was told to order the creamed corn," Jackson said, eyeing the grayish-yellow muck boiling in a pan next to some off-color green beans.

The lunch lady cocked a bushy eyebrow. "Did you say you wanted the creamed corn?"

"Yes, the creamed corn."

"You sure, kid? Once you have the creamed corn, there's no going back."

Jackson shook some toilet water out of his ear. "I'm sure."

The lunch lady scooped out a heaping helping of the goop and plopped it onto Jackson's tray. "Welcome to the team, kid," she said.

Once he found a seat, Jackson took a sniff of the corn and quickly realized that ordering it had been a terrible decision. It smelled like feet and maple syrup, and jiggled on the tray as if it were alive. Summoning all his courage and tightening all his stomach muscles, Jackson plunged his spoon into the goop and shoveled some into his mouth. Just as it went in, he thought he spotted something tiny and metallic. It was too late. He had already swallowed.

Jackson could feel the metal thing at the back of his throat, but it wasn't sinking into his stomach, it was climbing into his nasal cavity! There was an odd tickling feeling and then a sudden sharp pain that made Jackson yelp, which made every kid in the cafeteria look in his direction.

There was horrible popping sound and then Jackson's head filled with a whining feedback. He clamped his hands on his ears and cried out in agony. He heard a kid sitting behind him diagnose him as a lunatic. He was about to reply when he heard another voice, this one soft and calming.

"Welcome, Braceface."

"Hello?"

"Do you wish to join NERDS, Braceface? Please confirm."

Jackson nodded. "Sure . . . I guess. But my name is Jackson—"

"Yes or no is required, Braceface."

"Enough with the Braceface! Yes! I want to join," he shouted, collecting more bug-eyed gazes.

"Confirmed. You have received a TL-46A Tracking, Calling, and Communication Implant. It has three functions. The first emits a unique radio frequency allowing agents to track your whereabouts. I will test this function."

An incredible squeal blasted in Jackson's brain. The pain was similar to that of eating an ice cream cone too fast except, in this case, it was like eating forty pounds of ice cream too fast. Jackson's head was filled with a teeth-rattling screech and he fell over onto the floor. The kids who were sitting nearby picked up their trays and moved to other seats.

"Adjusting volume," the voice said as the noise faded. "The TL-46A's secondary function is as a pager system to alert agents of a crisis. I will test this function."

Just then, Jackson felt an incredible itch in his nose and he let out a massive sneeze. His nose was running like a river, and he wiped it on his sleeve. He had seen the same thing happen to the nerd herd.

"Secondary function working within parameters," the computer said. "OK, Braceface—"

"All right, pal, you call me Braceface one more time and I'm going to—"

"Testing."

Suddenly, Jackson's nose started to tickle and he sneezed. Then he sneezed again, and again, and again.

"Lastly, the implant allows communication between agents. Testing."

There was a horrible whine of feedback in his head that caused Jackson to slam his head on his table and hold his hands over his ears.

"Prepare to be delivered," Benjamin's voice continued.

"Delivered?"

Just then, the fire alarm rang and the sprinkler system came to life. Cold water poured down, causing panicked kids and staff to rush for the exits. In the chaos, Jackson felt the floor below him disappear, and he plummeted into darkness, landing in an overstuffed chair next to the computer desk in the center of the Playground. Agent Brand was waiting for him.

"Welcome to the team," Brand said, helping the boy to his feet. Jackson brushed himself off and scanned his surroundings. The scientists he had seen before were busy working on their various experiments.

"Well, I suppose we should get right to it," Brand continued as he escorted Jackson around the massive room. "You've seen the Playground before. It's our mission room, as well as a multifunction lab, information collection center, and training facility. You've met a few of our scientists. There are nearly fifty on staff, and they make up the finest minds in chemistry, engineering, and astrophysics—all working on the latest technologies to help your missions succeed."

Somewhere, something exploded.

Brand continued the tour, showing Jackson a bank of desks manned by men and women watching video monitors. "We also have a full team of experts who search the globe for trouble. Our eyes are everywhere, so that we can stop a problem before it starts. This is where missions start and end, Jackson."

The spy led him to a wall with a big red button on it. He

instructed Jackson to press his back against the wall, and then Brand pushed the button. The wall spun around, and they found themselves in a tight, confined space that smelled of body odor. The spy opened a door and the two stepped out into one of the school hallways. Jackson realized they had come back through another set of lockers—just as he had entered the Playground on the first day of his screwy new life.

They walked down the hallway to the library.

"I want you to meet our information specialist, Ms. Holiday."

"Ms. Holiday—you mean the librarian? She's a spy?" Jackson cried.

Agent Brand nodded. "She assists with mission intelligence, cover stories, clothing and weapons, and mission preparation. At the moment she's relaying the latest intelligence on an ongoing investigation to the team. Why don't we go in and say hello? I'm sure they will be thrilled to hear you've agreed to join them."

They stepped through the doorway and found Heathcliff, Ruby, Matilda, Duncan, and Flinch sitting at a round table. They looked angry.

Jackson was puzzled. Maybe they were angry about their mission, because surely, deep down, nerds would be honored to hang out with a kid like him. He turned to the nerds and smiled his best popular-kid smile. "Listen up, folks. I'm thrilled to be joining the team. Clearly, you needed someone with a little athletic ability, and it doesn't hurt that I'm cute and brimming with charm. I mean, you've seen those James Bond movies. He looks a lot more like me than he does the rest of you. So, I guess I'll be the face of the team and you guys can do whatever it is you do behind the scenes. Good? Good. Glad to be here."

Ms. Holiday rushed to Brand's side. She looked worried.

"Agent Brand, the team has something to say," she said.

Brand cocked an eyebrow. "Indeed?"

"We've taken a vote," Ruby said, and she jumped to her feet.

"A vote?" the spy asked.

"Yes. We have decided that this punk is not right for our team. He has no training. He is a show-off and I doubt he'll take orders. We have decided to pass."

Agent Brand's face tightened like he had just bitten into a very sour pickle.

"Pufferfish," the spy said. "I'm sure that once the six of you get to know one another—"

"We know everything we need to know about him," Heathcliff said.

"Hggggaalfhal amldyad aaaal," Flinch sputtered.

"What did he say?" the spy asked.

The hyper boy turned the knob on this harness and spoke again. "He's a jerk."

Suddenly, all the children were shouting angry words at Brand.

"Children!" Ms. Holiday cried over the chaos. "Let's be professional. Jackson has a lot to offer the team."

Matilda laughed. "He'll draw attention to himself and us. He can't help it. All he cares about is being popular."

Brand's face was hot and red. He looked as if he had a million things to say, but he gritted his teeth and said, "Train him." Then he turned and walked out of the room.

The team was quiet for a moment. It was clear to Jackson

they were unused to hearing someone tell them what to do. It was also clear they were very accustomed to getting their way.

Ms. Holiday forced a smile onto her face. "Welcome to the team, Braceface."

"Uh, can we talk about my code name?" Jackson said.

Ms. Holiday laughed, trying to break the mood. "I suppose we should get your training started. Matilda, why don't we start with you? Take Jackson down to the Playground and give him some hand-to-hand combat instruction."

"I refuse," Matilda wheezed.

She reminded Jackson of a small, squeaky toy that Butch the dog liked to chew. Jackson laughed. "Good, because Ms. Holiday, you should really have someone strong and fast teach me, not this little girl."

"On second thought . . ." Matilda smiled slyly then turned to the librarian. "What's the rule on broken bones?"

Ms. Holiday frowned. "The rule is there can't be any broken bones," she scolded.

Matilda frowned. "You're no fun."

SUPPLEMENTAL INFORMATION: TRAINING RESULTS FOR BRACEFACE
FIRST INSTRUCTOR: WHEEZER

Matilda led Jackson back through the Playground and into one of the many rooms that lined the main room. She pulled the door closed, and a series of heavy locks turned and sealed them inside. Suddenly, the walls flipped over, revealing a variety of weapons.

"We call this the supply closet. We come here to learn to fight and defend ourselves. I spend at least four hours a day here honing my combat skills."

Matilda took a hit of her inhaler.

"Honing your combat skills?" Jackson chuckled. "You look like you need help getting out of bed."

"That's exactly what makes me a great secret agent. No one suspects I can kick butt. I'll show you. Pick a weapon and attack me with it."

"Forget that. I'm not going to hit a girl."

Matilda's inhalers blasted hot flames and she rose several feet off the ground. "Good, then this will be a lot easier for me." The littlest of the spies shot forward and clotheslined Jackson across the chest. He crashed onto his back and cried out in agony.

Once his head cleared, he turned to Matilda. "I wouldn't do that again if I were you."

Matilda soared across the room, reached down with one arm, and bodyslammed him back to the floor. Jackson's lungs burned. He slowly got to his feet. This time his fists were clenched.

"Are you nuts?"

"Are *you*?" Matilda asked as she spun around like a ballerina in the air and landed on his shoulders. She slammed the flats of her hands against his ears, sending a shock of pain into his brain. "I'm beating you senseless and you're just taking it."

Jackson staggered about and waited for the ringing in his skull to subside. While he was recovering, Matilda floated back down to the floor.

"Grab a weapon and fight back."

"I'm not going to hit a girl!" Jackson repeated.

Matilda twisted his arm around his back and held it there. The agony in his shoulder felt like a bonfire and, worse, he was helpless.

"So, if you come face-to-face with a major-league bad guy who happens to be a girl, you're going to let her kill you?"

She wrapped her arm around his neck, pushed forward, and slammed him face-first into the hard floor. "I call that a bulldog," she said proudly as she rose back into the air. She flew around him, circling like a hungry hawk.

"That's your problem, Braceface. You judge others by what they look like. You've spent your life putting people into little categories—nerd, geek, athlete, cheerleader, weakling—and you can't imagine they might be more than what you think. People are always more than what they appear. You have a lazy mind, kid, and it's going to get you killed one of these days."

She turned one of her inhalers on him and a blast of energy hit him in the belly, knocking the wind out of him.

"Fine, you want to fight? Let's do this!" Jackson cried when he could breathe again. Without looking, Jackson reached behind him and snatched a weapon off the wall. When he saw what it was, he frowned—a bamboo back scratcher. He turned for a new weapon, but the walls flipped over and the weapons were gone.

"Hey!"

"One weapon at a time, chump," Matilda said, landing in front of him.

"That's not fair! Let me pick again!"

Matilda shook her head. "Now you're putting the weapons in categories. A good secret agent can use anything as a weapon. A back scratcher can be just as deadly as a chain saw. It shouldn't matter what you choose. I once took out a dozen terrorists with a jelly donut and a cup of cocoa."

She spun around like a top, then kicked him in the arm.

In anger, he lashed out with the back scratcher, but Matilda pressed the plungers on her inhalers and soared out of his reach, easily dodging the blow. Startled, Jackson left his defenses wide open, and Matilda kicked him in the ribs. Enraged, Jackson slashed at the flying girl. Unfortunately, he only managed to hit himself in the ear.

Matilda landed again. She studied Jackson with pity. "Fine. I'll take the back scratcher. You take another weapon," she said, then clapped her hands twice. The walls flipped over and the weapons reappeared.

Jackson raised a suspicious eyebrow. "Really?"

Matilda held out her hand. Jackson passed her the back scratcher and eagerly scanned the walls for something, anything, that would get Matilda to stop kicking his butt. There were pitchforks, nunchakus, sabers, throwing stars, bazookas, spears, and crossbows. Finally he spotted what he needed—a Louisville Slugger! He yanked it off the wall, knowing he'd never hit Matilda with it, but he thought perhaps she'd be intimidated enough to back off.

He turned to Matilda. She was spinning the back scratcher in her hands like a baton. "I'll even let you go first."

"Your funeral," Jackson said as he stomped toward her. He tried to swing the bat but never got the chance. Matilda brought the scratcher down on his nose so hard tears welled in his eyes and blinded him. Helpless to her assault, Jackson cowered as Matilda slapped him in the lips, on top of his head, and then on his Adam's apple. Next she went to work on his chest, his elbows, his belly, his rump, and finally his knees. As he gasped for breath, he saw the small girl fly into the air, spin around in a circle like a cyclone, and then plant her foot on his jaw. The last thing he saw before he blacked out was Matilda standing over him with a proud smile.

"I love this job," she said.

RESULTS: FAILURE

SUPPLEMENTAL INFORMATION: TRAINING RESULTS FOR BRACEFACE

SECOND INSTRUCTOR: CHOPPERS

After a serious smackdown from Matilda, Jackson was instructed to meet Heathcliff at the far end of the school building, on a tiny playground reserved for kindergartners. Heathcliff had a smug grin on his face that even his enormous buckteeth couldn't hide.

"What are we doing here?" Jackson asked.

"Trust me, it's not my idea. I wouldn't help you if it weren't a direct order. I'm supposed to train you to deal with an unpredictable situation." Heathcliff's disdain for Jackson dripped from every word. "A good secret agent must be prepared for anything. It's the ability to think on your feet that will keep you alive."

"Well, I don't want to brag, but I saw a lot of unpredictable situations when I was leading the Tigers to the state championship. I don't think your little training session will be much of a challenge."

Just then, a bell rang and the door flew open. A sea of five-year-olds flooded the playground. They were as hyper as Flinch after a fluffernutter sandwich, and they ran about screaming, kicking balls, chasing each other, and singing like maniacs.

"What's this all about?" Jackson said, trying to avoid a soccer ball to the head.

"You'll see," Heathcliff said as he turned to the children and smiled, flashing his giant teeth. "Get him, kids!"

The children stared at Heathcliff like he was as transfixing as a talking ice cream cone, then grew very still. All at once, they whipped their heads in Jackson's direction and screamed in anger.

"Have fun," Heathcliff shouted as the children rushed toward Jackson. With balls, jacks, rocks, and lunch boxes, they rained fury down on Jackson.

He was stunned at first. No one expects to be attacked by a bunch of hypnotized five-year-olds, but that was exactly what was happening. When a NASCAR lunch box cracked him in the skull, he knew he had to defend himself. But how? He didn't feel right about fighting back, especially since the children were not in their right minds. He wondered if his braces could help. He tried to focus on the metal in his mouth, and suddenly it was swirling. A moment later, four long tentacles emerged from his lips, dipped down to the ground, and lifted him into the air, making him into a human spider. He picked his tentacled way through the crowd of children, but his escape only seemed to enrage them more. They chased after him, flinging their toys at his back, and shouting threats.

Worse still, he couldn't outrun them. No matter which direction the legs carried him, the children were right behind, their hypnotized faces twisted in rage. He made a dash across the playground. Suddenly, his metallic legs tripped and he fell face-first into a set of monkey bars. His braces were tied up, and no matter what he did, he could not free them. It was the break the zombie children needed, and they fell on him with jump ropes, dollies, and finger paints. As they beat him senseless, he could see Heathcliff standing over him, laughing.

RESULTS: FAILURE

SUPPLEMENTAL INFORMATION: TRAINING RESULTS FOR BRACEFACE

THIRD INSTRUCTOR: GLUESTICK

When Jackson could walk again, he staggered over to the older kids' playground, where Duncan was waiting.

"What happened to you?" the chubby boy asked.

Jackson frowned and waved off the question. "I'd rather not talk about it. What's next?"

Duncan gestured to a tetherball pole and led Jackson to it.

"We're going to play tetherball?" Jackson asked hopefully.

"Not exactly," Duncan said. He reached into his pocket and took out what looked like a remote control. He pushed a button and the tetherball lifted off the chain like the head of a curious snake. "The tetherball is going to play you."

"What's all this?"

Duncan flashed a knowing smile. "I'm here to teach you the fine art of stealth, or in layman's terms, how to be sneaky. A good secret agent needs to be able to operate in the shadows, move undetected, and keep a low profile. I suspect you'll have problems with this."

"Oh yeah?"

Duncan nodded. "You're what my father would call a showboat. In today's slang, I'd call you a glory hog. Think you can step out of your spotlight for a bit?"

Jackson scowled. "Let's just do this."

Duncan pushed another button on the remote, and the tetherball whipped around and snapped the chain that held it. Then it floated into the air above them. "This is the XP-400 Surveillance and Attack Sphere. I could talk for hours about its design—"

"I bet you could."

Duncan ignored the interruption. "But to hurry this along, I'll give you a brief explanation. You are going to hide somewhere in the school. This ball is going to find you. When it finds you, it's going to shoot you with a high-intensity laser. It will hurt. A lot."

"A laser?"

Duncan cocked an eyebrow. "Yes, Jackson. Are you afraid of a little ball? I thought you were an athlete. I read in the school paper that you hold our school's all-time passing record. Now, I don't know what that means, but I assume it means you're fast. You can probably beat this thing, but if you're scared . . ."

Jackson was aware of how reverse psychology worked. After all, he had once had a mother. But the boy's tone made him angry. This chubby jerk was questioning his athletic prowess.

He had to prove him wrong. "Try to catch me, porky," he shouted as he turned and raced into the school.

"Good luck!" Duncan shouted. "You're going to need it."

Jackson suspected his best chance of avoiding the laser ball was to find a room and lock himself inside. The XP-400 couldn't zap what it couldn't get to, and Jackson knew the perfect place: the library. He sprinted down the hall, threw open the library door, and closed it behind him. As he caught his breath, he smiled proudly. Finally, he had outsmarted one of these so-called spies—and it had been easy. Maybe these *nerds* weren't good enough to be on a team with *him*. He sat down at a table, kicked up his feet, and contemplated a nap. That was until he saw something he would never have believed possible. The door to the library suddenly grew bright red, and a moment later it exploded. Chunks of wood and metal flew in all directions, and the library filled with a thick, black smoke. The explosion knocked Jackson out of his chair. He scrambled to his feet as the menacing orange ball floated into the room. Before he could dash away to a better hiding spot, the XP-400 fired and stung him in the rear. It felt like he had been bitten by a shark and he screamed in agony. Instinctively, Jackson leaped behind a shelf of books and rubbed his sore behind.

"I told you it would hurt," Duncan said. Jackson scanned

the room for the chubby spy and spotted him walking along the ceiling, leaving a trail of sticky footprints.

Jackson sprinted out of the room ahead of another laser shot. He ran down the hall and darted into the cafeteria. It dawned on him that he had not taken Duncan seriously. The nerd had mentioned that this was a test of stealth—not the ability to hide behind a door. Maybe the fat toad knew what he was talking about. As Jackson peered around the room, a stack of trays exploded behind him and showered down on his head. He leaped behind a table and tried to calm his breathing. It was then that he realized he could hear the machine. It made a subtle but audible hum. It was getting closer and would be on him in no time. He had to do something—and fast. It was then he recalled an old saying often used in his PeeWee football league: "Distraction wins games." He leaped to his feet, snatched one of the trays from the ground, and tossed it to his right. He heard the sphere dart after the tray, so he dashed in the opposite direction. He was safely behind another table before the floating ball could react.

"Stupid machine." Jackson chuckled.

"Hey, Jackson," Duncan shouted. He was walking along the wall.

"I'm beating your ball," Jackson shouted back.

"I forgot to tell you something," he said. "The sphere can replicate itself."

"It can do what?"

"It can make copies of itself!" the nerd shouted.

Suddenly, the humming grew louder and louder. Jackson looked up. Ten tetherballs hovered over his head, and moments later, the lasers fired.

RESULTS: FAILURE

SUPPLEMENTAL INFORMATION: TRAINING RESULTS FOR BRACEFACE
FOURTH INSTRUCTOR: FLINCH

Jackson met Flinch in the parking lot of the school. The nerd's face was covered in caramel, and there were a dozen or so candy bar wrappers lying at his feet. He had a cup of convenience store soda in his hand that was bigger than his own head. He was also trembling with caffeinated joy.

"So, I suppose you're going to beat me up too," Jackson said. He could still feel the burning laser stings on his behind, the bruises from the back scratcher, and the place where the kindergartener's lunch box had hit him in the skull.

Flinch shook his head wildly. It seemed everything he did was over the top. "No way! We're going to play a game of catch, bro."

"Catch? OK, that's something I'm very good at," Jackson said.

"But you're going to use your superbraces to do it," Flinch said. "All that technology in your mouth is awesome! We have to teach you how to use it. Luckily, a lot of it is responsive to what's going on around you. Here, I'll show you."

Jackson watched Flinch step over to a teacher's car. He turned the dial on his harness and then, in one swift motion,

leaned down and picked the car up off the ground. He held it over his head like it was a feather pillow. Then he tossed it at Jackson.

Jackson screamed and instinctively ducked, though he knew it wouldn't do much to prevent his impending death. What he couldn't have imagined was the braces in his mouth springing to life. They forced his mouth open and several strands of metal caught the car in midair.

"Hombre, that is awesome," Flinch shouted. "Throw it back."

Jackson didn't have time to think before the braces hefted the car back at the little boy. Flinch snatched it out of the air and set it back down in its parking space.

"You just threw a car at me!" Jackson yelled.

"Fun, isn't it?" Flinch shouted as he shoved a peanut butter cup into his mouth.

"Fun is not the word I would use to describe it," Jackson replied.

"Heads up!" Flinch shouted as he tossed another of the teachers' cars at him. This time the braces seemed ready and stopped it long before it closed in on his head. Still, the experience was heart-attack inducing. Jackson set the car down just in time to spot another sailing through the air at him.

"Cut it out!" Jackson shouted as he caught it and set it back on its four wheels.

"I'm strong like bull!" Flinch shouted, oblivious to Jackson's complaints. "Let's make this interesting."

He snatched a car, tossed it, then snatched another, then tossed it, and on and on and on. The cars sailed through the air fast and furious. Jackson's braces spun around in his mouth like a blender as they attempted to catch them all, but there were too many. The best he could do was try to swat them away. His efforts did little, and soon one of the cars crashed to the ground next to him. Then another landed right behind. Soon the cars were piling up around him, locking him inside an automotive pyramid. He was safe and unharmed, but he was trapped.

"You are supposed to catch them," Flinch shouted.

Jackson stewed with anger. "Get me out of here, you freak!"

RESULTS: FAILURE

Flinch pulled Jackson out of the car pyramid and told him to go back inside. As painful, humiliating, and downright scary as his experiences had been that day, they faded in comparison to the nerve-racking tension of meeting Ruby Peet. Pufferfish hadn't exactly hidden the fact that she hated him.

Much to Jackson's surprise, the only things in the room in which he found her were a small black box with several suction cups attached to it, a desk, and two chairs.

"Why don't you have a seat?" she said.

"So, what's all this?" he said apprehensively.

Ruby smiled and attached the little suction cups to Jackson's temples. "Nothing to worry about. I know the others have been a little rough on you, but I can assure you that nothing in this room will hurt you."

"Good."

"Unless you tell a lie," Ruby said.

"Oh, is this one of those lie detectors?" Jackson said, eyeing the little black box once more. He noticed it was plugged into the electrical socket on the wall.

"No, I'm the lie detector. I'm allergic to lying," Ruby said.

Jackson giggled. "Allergic to lying. That's hilarious."

Ruby smiled. "The point of this exercise is to train you to stay calm under pressure and teach you how to tell a lie effectively. A good spy is called upon to lie from time to time. If you have valuable information, you will need to convince our enemies that you don't know anything. You may have to lie to save a life. You may have to lie to save the world. Lying is a skill that takes a lot of practice. This machine will help you hone this talent."

"How?"

"Every time you tell a lie and I detect it, it's going to send volts of electricity through your body. Ready to get started?"

Jackson winced and nodded.

"Is your name Jackson Jones?"

Jackson smiled. "Yes."

"Very good," Ruby said. "You're telling the truth. Are you a student at Nathan Hale Elementary?"

"Duh! I was only one of the most popular kids in the history of the school," Jackson said.

"Very good," Ruby said.

"Jackson, have you ever kissed a girl?"

Jackson hesitated. "Of course I have."

Jackson watched as Ruby's right arm swelled to the size of a watermelon. She scratched at it furiously. "You lied." She pushed a button on the black box and a blast of electricity hit Jackson.

"Ouch!"

"Next question," Ruby said. "Did you play for the school's football team?"

"Yes," Jackson grumbled.

"Good," Ruby said. "Does your father write your name on your underwear?"

"Of course not," Jackson cried.

Ruby face and neck broke out into bright red hives. A second later there was another shock.

"Jackson, have you ever wet the bed?"

Jackson blinked.

"Do I need to repeat the question?"

"I refuse to answer."

"You can't. You have to say yes or no. I'll shock you if you don't."

Sweat dotted Jackson's face, but he did what he could to calm down. He closed his eyes, took deep breaths, and relaxed his beating heart. Then, when he was feeling serene, he opened his eyes. "The answer is no."

Ruby stared at him for a long time, but she did not scratch herself. In fact, she looked perfectly comfortable.

"You're not lying."

Jackson shook his head. "I've never wet the bed. Ever."

"Hmmmm," Ruby said. "OK, let's move on to the next question."

"Aha! I beat your lie detector," Jackson bragged.

Suddenly, Ruby's eyes started to water and her feet swelled so much she ripped through her shoes. Her nose ran like a river and her lips puffed up so much that they looked as if they had been attacked by a swarm of honeybees.

"*Liar!*" she shouted as her swollen thumb slammed the shock button. For three days after the test, Jackson felt as if he had been microwaved like a baked potato.

RESULTS: FAILURE

END TRANSMISSION.

WELL, WELL, WELL—YOU'RE STILL HERE. PERSEVERANCE IS A BIG PART OF JOINING THE TEAM. PERSONALLY, I WOULD HAVE BET MONEY YOU'D HAVE RUN HOME TO YOUR MOMMY BY NOW. ANYWAY, YOU NEED LEVEL 5 CLEARANCE TO READ FURTHER, AND TO GET LEVEL 5 CLEARANCE YOU NEED TO GIVE A SALIVA SAMPLE. PLEASE LICK THE SENSOR.

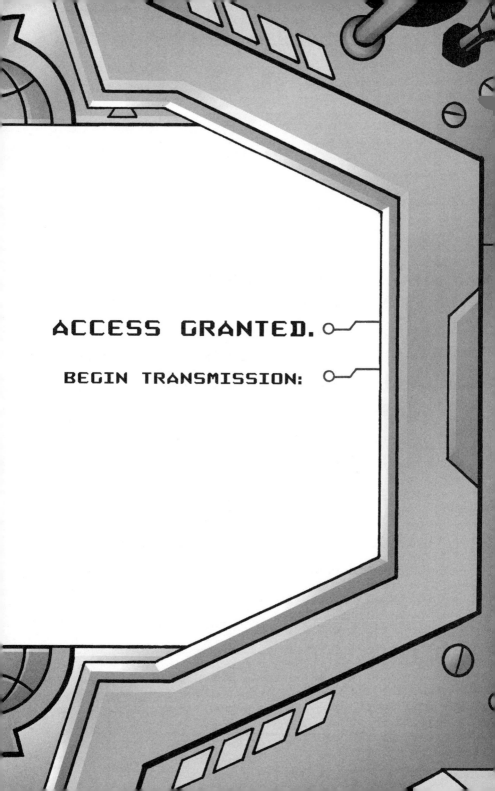

10

90° N

The Hyena was surprised when Dumb Vinci told her that Dr. Jigsaw wanted to see her in his secret lab, where his henchmen still worked day and night on the giant satellite dish. She asked the goon what Jigsaw wanted, but he couldn't elaborate, so she grabbed her warmest sweater and headed toward the scientist's inner lair.

Once inside, the Hyena wished she had worn a coat. Jigsaw, however, seemed oblivious to the cold. He was wearing just a thin lab jacket and a scarf. He smiled and gestured for her to follow him. He led her up a flight of stairs to a tiny room looking out over the lab. Inside was a chair, a desk, a computer, and thousands of jigsaw puzzle pieces, covering the floor. The box for the puzzle was tacked on the wall. It showed a map of the world. Jigsaw scooped up a handful of pieces and snatched a pair of scissors off the desk, then he stood by the window overlooking the lab and gazed down on his machine.

"You have done well, Mindy," he said. The Hyena bristled at the use of her real name, but kept her cool. Jigsaw was paying the bills. He could call her Señorita Monkeyface if he wanted. "Lunich's invention is an essential element of my design," Jigsaw continued. "Without it we might have suffered setbacks. Simon doesn't like setbacks."

"Who is Simon?" the Hyena asked.

Jigsaw ignored her. "Mindy, do you know the definition of beauty?"

"I'm not sure what you mean, sir."

"Beauty," Jigsaw repeated. He used the scissors to cut the jigsaw pieces into entirely new shapes, as if he was unhappy with the picture the puzzle was making. What he had completed so far didn't look much like the Earth. "It's a simple question."

"Beauty is something that's visually appealing," the Hyena answered.

"A simple answer for a simple question. Some might argue that beauty is more than what you see, that it involves a variety of senses—smell, sound, and touch, as well as vision. All combining to represent what many people might label as beauty."

The Hyena was confused but said nothing. She could tell that Jigsaw was making his I'm-an-evil-mastermind speech. He would find it rude if she interrupted with questions.

"Still others subscribe to a notion that beauty is defined by perfect symmetry," the scientist continued. "Have you heard that word before?"

The Hyena nodded. "That's when things balance each other."

"Very true. Take a human being. What we often call beauty is no more than features that align; eyes that are just the right

width apart, a nose that doesn't sit too low on a face, high, perfectly matched cheekbones. Symmetry is what makes beauty possible. It creates the ideal. It's at the heart of nature. But what happens when symmetry hasn't been provided, or worse, has been broken? The beauty is distorted. It's impossible to see clearly. When that happens, at least for the human animal, we turn to surgeons who can give us what nature has not provided. What a noble profession that must be—surgeon."

"Uh, yeah," the Hyena said. She tried not to stare at Jigsaw's face-lift. It looked as if someone had collected his loose skin and tied it into a knot on the back of his head. It was distracting.

"I like to think of myself as a surgeon," Jigsaw continued. "In many ways what my machine and I are doing is reconstructive surgery. I thought you might like to see a demonstration."

Jigsaw tapped a button on a speaker near his window. "Is the new tractor beam ready?"

A crackling voice replied, "Yes, sir."

"Lock in coordinates."

"Coordinates are ready, sir," the voice said.

"You have a 'go,'" Jigsaw replied.

There was a loud blasting sound and the Hyena watched the giant satellite dish turn toward another part of the sky. Mounted on the dish was a huge peg-shaped object. The Hyena recognized it at once. It was a gigantic version of Dr. Lunich's tiny invention. Jigsaw and the scientists had figured out how it worked! Jigsaw clapped like a happy baby and led the Hyena to the computer in the far corner of the room. On the screen was a satellite map of the world. He pointed to the Hawaiian Islands and grinned. "Have you ever been to Hawaii, Mindy?"

The Hyena nodded.

"Lovely place," Jigsaw said. "Though it's quite expensive to go there and the flight is very long. I've always wished that wasn't the case."

Just then there was a loud rumbling sound from the lab below. The dish was glowing with energy, and when the Hyena was sure it was about to explode, a green beam shot into the air.

"Watch the monitor, Mindy," Jigsaw said.

She turned back to the computer and watched as the satellite image revealed something that the Hyena was sure was impossible. The entire chain of Hawaiian Islands began to move. It drifted toward the coast of California and stopped somewhere near San Francisco.

The henchman's voice chirped through the speaker. "Sir, congratulations! The test was a success," the voice replied.

"I'm pleased, and Simon will be too," Jigsaw replied.

"Unfortunately, the fuel cell on the dish has been destroyed. To finish your plans we're going to need a power source with nearly unlimited energy."

"And very soon I will provide you with the next element of the machine's design. It will fix all of our problems," Jigsaw said. Then he turned off the speaker box and faced his puzzle. He snatched his scissors and went to work cutting out new jigsaw puzzle pieces.

11

38°53 N, 77°05 W

"Mr. Jones, I'm sick of seeing your face in my office!" Mr. Dehaven shouted as Jackson sat in a chair before him.

"I'm sick of being here," Jackson grumbled to himself. Since he had joined the NERDS, Jackson had been in Dehaven's office seven times.

"You have been late for school every day for two weeks. Why is that?"

Jackson rolled through a list of previously constructed lies: he was attacked by dogs, the power went out and his alarm clock didn't go off, his house burned down, etc. Jackson wanted to tell Dehaven the truth. He wanted to tell him that he hadn't been getting enough sleep because he was busy learning to fight and be sneaky and to interrogate suspects, and reading through mountains of files and reports on every little squabble anyone had ever had for the last twenty years. He wanted to tell him everything so Dehaven would get off his back, but he couldn't. He had been sworn to secrecy.

"I know exactly why you're late every day," Dehaven barked.

Jackson felt a bead of sweat roll down his face. "You do?"

"I do. You're late because you have no respect for anyone or anything other than yourself. You're lazy and shiftless, and won't amount to much. Unfortunately, I am required by law to keep trying to reach out to you so that you know what a wonderful gift an education can be. And I assure you, you're going to appreciate it whether you like it or not. Now, what are we going to do about this problem, Mr. Jones? Hmmm?"

"I'm not sure. I probably need to think about it," Jackson said.

"I couldn't agree more. Thinking about it is exactly what you should do and the best place to do that is in detention. How about two weeks?"

"Two weeks!" Jackson cried.

"See, there's an old saying, son. When you mess with the bull, you get the horns. I'm the bull, Mr. Jones." Jackson watched as Dehaven made horns on the side of his head with his fingers.

Jackson shuffled down the hall feeling as if the whole world were on his shoulders. Since joining the team, his grades had plummeted, his teachers looked at him like he was a degenerate, and his father was considering sending him to military school.

On top of that, he was blowing it big time with his training. He was getting better at some things. He'd managed to avoid the tetherball for almost ten minutes and caught a few more Toyotas with his braces, but the kindergarteners were still beating him senseless, he hadn't fooled Ruby's lie detection once, and Matilda had pummeled him with an egg timer, a Whiffle ball bat, a ream of copy paper, and a jar of dill pickles in the span of a week. He was sure Agent Brand would kick him off the team at any moment.

As he slipped Mr. Pfeiffer his tardy note, he wondered if he was cut out to be a secret agent. It was so much work and the team expected nothing but perfection. He wished he could go back to his old life, when he was popular and carefree. He sat down and listened to Pfeiffer prattle on about online dating and quietly envied the man. Pfeiffer had no idea what was happening at this school, and he was happy. Ignorance was bliss.

At that moment, he felt a strong tingle in his nose, and let loose with an explosive sneeze. A second later, he was following the rest of the team toward the lockers that led to the Playground.

"What's going on?" he asked.

Duncan responded. He was the only one who would talk to Jackson outside of training. "Probably a mission."

Jackson stepped into the locker he'd been assigned by Brand.

As usual, the floor disappeared and he was tossed around in the secret tubes, landing at last in the Playground, on his rump. The others, naturally, landed on their feet.

"Please take your seats, agents," Brand said as he gestured to the circular desk in the center of the room. As everyone was getting settled, Ms. Holiday arrived. She looked nervous and worried, and stood off to the side while chewing on a fingernail. When everyone was settled, Brand waved his hand over the blue orb, which brought it to life.

"Benjamin, we're ready for our briefing," Brand said.

Benjamin's voice filled the room. "Of course, Agent Brand."

The orb sent flecks of light dancing around the room. After a moment, they came together to reveal a series of photographs.

Brand spoke. "As you know, we've been tracking several kidnappings in the scientific community. The number of big brains that have been abducted is growing by the day. Dr. Robert Hill, a preeminent geologist; Dr. Judy Pray, an expert on tides and water movement; Dr. Francis Pizzani, a specialist in antigravitational devices; and, lastly, Dr. Joseph Lunich, who recently invented something called the miniature tractor beam."

"It's truly a marvelous device," Duncan said. "It has hundreds of practical applications."

"As usual, Gluestick is ahead of us all," Brand said. "Yes, Dr. Lunich is missing, as is one of his prototypes."

Matilda took a hit off her inhaler. "Who is doing the kidnapping?"

"We don't have a clue," Ms. Holiday said with a sigh. "But we did retrieve this at the scene of the last kidnapping. It was found next to an expensive black boot."

A copy of a yellow list appeared before them. The names Brand had just listed were crossed off, but there was one that still hadn't been touched. "We believe whoever is doing the goon work left this behind."

"Could this have something to do with all the crazy moving islands?" Flinch said as he sucked the cream filling out of a cupcake with a straw.

"My thoughts as well," Brand said. "That's why we're taking over these kidnapping cases. Normally, this is a job for the FBI, but if the events are somehow connected, then it's more than the feds can handle."

"So all the scientists have been crossed off but one," Ruby said. "Who's the lucky person?"

Ms. Holiday ran her hand over the orb and a photograph of a middle-aged woman with dark skin and a thin face appeared. "Dr. Nashwa Badawi—a mineralogist who discovered a rare substance that can be used in supercharged solar power collectors. Her work has countless commercial and military applications. I'm told that one five-foot panel matches the fuel output of a nuclear power plant. It's clean and cheap, too. Badawi may very well have created a fuel source for the next generation!"

"Geology, solar power, tidal movement—whoever is behind this is obviously up to something big, and whatever it is, it can't be good," Ruby said.

"We've got analysts trying to figure out what it might be, but for now we have to make sure that Dr. Badawi is safe," Ms. Holiday explained.

"So we're bodyguards now?" Heathcliff asked.

Brand ignored the sarcasm in the boy's voice. "Our mission is to outmaneuver the bad guys. We're going to kidnap Dr. Badawi before they can."

Ruby sat back in her chair, stunned. "Kidnap her?"

Brand nodded. "If we pick her up and hide her, it puts a stop to whoever is behind this list. We did this many times when I worked for the Special Operations Bureau. Ms. Holiday has more about the mission."

Brand turned and walked away.

"He's not what I'd call a chatty guy," Jackson said.

Ms. Holiday gave a knowing smile. She straightened her glasses and skirt, and placed her hand on a panel near the spinning blue orb. The images faded and were replaced by a scene of a desert. "The Nile River Valley in Egypt is a dry one hundred and two degrees today—"

"Wait! We're going to Egypt?" Jackson cried. "I can't go to Egypt! I've got detention."

The group stared at him as if he were a babbling idiot.

"I'm serious," Jackson said. "I'm in big trouble. My grades are falling and Dehaven has decided to make me his personal project."

Heathcliff shot him a disgusted look. "You're going to have to figure out how to solve your school problems on your own, Braceface."

Ms. Holiday continued her presentation. "Your ultimate destination is Cairo, the capital city of Egypt. It has a population of nearly seventeen million, so it's going to be pretty crowded. It's also a dangerous place. The government is in a state of flux, and religious zealots are struggling for control. Westerners are still welcome, but they aren't always respected or left alone. You'll have to be careful."

"When do we leave?" Matilda asked.

"Now," a voice said from behind them. Jackson turned and saw the lunch lady. "Let's get to the School Bus!"

The children and Ms. Holiday followed the lunch lady down a hallway. Jackson had concerns. "Um, I don't know a lot of about geography, but I know we can't drive to Cairo in a school bus."

The others ignored him and stepped through sliding doors

that led to a passageway. At the end of the passage, Jackson saw they were inside the school's gymnasium. Agent Brand was waiting for them in the center of the room. He stood near a rope hanging from the ceiling. Jackson knew the rope well. He held the school time record for climbing. Brand pulled on it three times and a violent rumbling rose from beneath Jackson. A huge section of the gym's floor slid aside, and from below an incredible machine rose. As it came into view, Jackson understood what it was—a rocket. It was bright orange and had small wings at the bottom. Once it was fully up, a dozen scientists in jumpsuits attached an enormous hose to its side. A moment later, the odor of fuel flooded Jackson's nose.

"What's that?" Jackson asked.

"That is the TA-48 Orbital Jet," the lunch lady said proudly. "But we call it the School Bus."

There was a loud siren wailing from speakers mounted on the wall. A moment later, Jackson could hear a voice beckoning all students to the basement because of a tornado warning.

"There isn't a cloud in the sky," Jackson said.

"True," the lunch lady replied. "But getting everyone into a crouched position in the basement distracts them for a while."

"Let's get that roof retracted, people," Brand shouted, and in no time there was more rumbling, this time from above. Jackson saw the gymnasium roof spreading apart, revealing the blue sky.

Ms. Holiday ushered the children up a small flight of stairs to

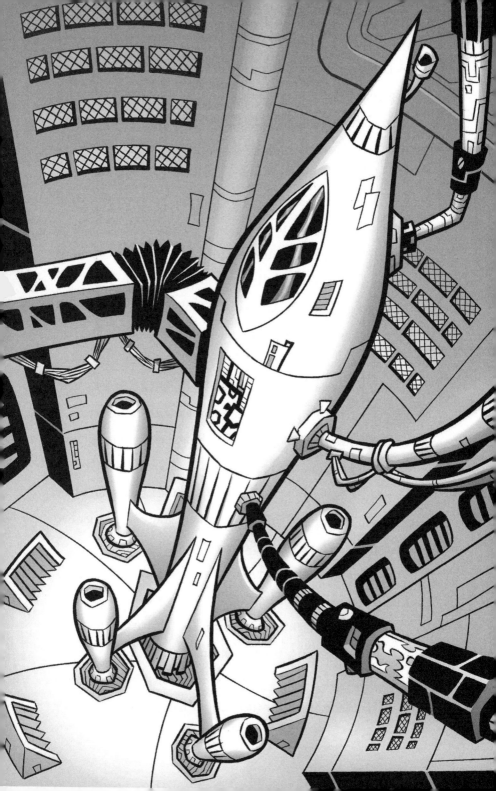

the rocket's door. "Come along. We have to get you on board."

"On board!" Jackson exclaimed. "I can't fly in a rocket."

Heathcliff, Duncan, Matilda, Ruby, and Flinch eyed him with disgust.

"It's always about you," Ruby said as the rest of the team entered the hull of the ship. Jackson reluctantly followed. Brand and Holiday brought up the rear.

Duncan rubbed his hands together eagerly as he strapped himself into one of eight leather seats. "I love missions!"

"Do I get to blow something up?" Matilda asked.

"That remains to be seen," Brand replied, helping the librarian into her seat and then taking his own.

A group of workers brought in six stuffed backpacks. Ms. Holiday smiled. "Oh, good, do they have everything?"

One of the workers nodded. "Everything that was on your list."

"You can put those in the storage compartment," Ms. Holiday said. The men opened a panel at the front of the jet and shoved the packs inside. A moment later the men were gone. No sooner had they left than the lunch lady climbed aboard.

"You ready to get this bird in the air?" she asked.

Brand nodded.

"She's the pilot? That woman can't make meat loaf. How is she going to fly a rocket?"

The lunch lady reached up and snatched her dull brown hair off her head. Jackson quickly realized she had been wearing a wig and had a clean-shaven bald head underneath. Then it dawned on him that the lunch lady wasn't a lady at all.

"You don't like my meat loaf, kid?" the lunch lady grunted. "I'm hurt."

"Buckle up," Ms. Holiday said.

Jackson considered jumping up and rushing out the open door while he still had a chance. Unfortunately, one of the workers slammed it shut. There was a loud roar and a sudden burst of speed, which caused Jackson to sink into his seat.

"Blast off!" Flinch cried. Jackson was horrified. He could feel the skin on his face clinging to his skull as it was pulled backward by the g-force, and he imagined the whole machine exploding. He turned to his window only to see the ship shoot out of the top of the school and rise higher and higher in the sky, up into the blackness of space. If he craned his neck, he could see the entire planet below. That's when Jackson screamed.

And screamed . . .

. . . and screamed.

"Oh boy," Heathcliff said, rolling his eyes. "I think we have a barfer on our hands."

END TRANSMISSION.

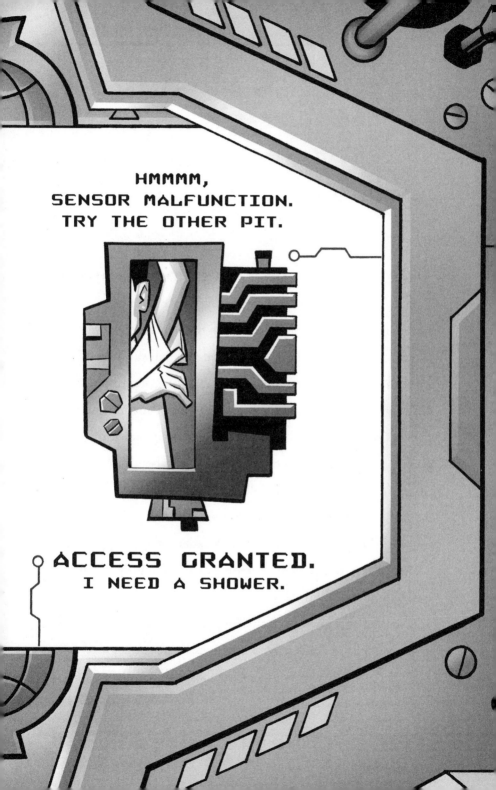

12

The halls of the Milwaukee Mental Hospital were a creepy place late at night. They were dim, with ominous shadows that slithered about in the moonlight. The rooms that lined the hallway were filled with the criminally insane—certifiable lunatics responsible for mayhem, murder, and quite a number of maimings. The patients were the incorrigiblest of the incorrigible, and if one were to break out of his room, there would be no predicting what kind of chaos would follow. The possibilities unnerved Denny Parsons. Sure, he was a trained security guard. He had a badge. He had a nightstick. But crazy people were crazy people and it didn't help that his partner, Tommy Newton, was a complete idiot.

"Look at this guy!" Tommy shouted as he peered through a window in one of the doors. "This guy is crazy."

"That's why they call this a mental hospital," Denny said.

"I know that," Tommy snapped. "But this one is real crazy.

He's in there flapping his arms like a duck. Hey, man, you ain't no duck! You can't fly!"

Denny wondered if Tommy would be missed if he were to somehow find himself locked in one of the rooms—maybe one of the soundproof ones with padded walls.

"Check this loony tune out," Tommy said as he moved to another room. "He's in there talking to himself. Hey! Ain't nobody in there talking to you! I tell you, Denny, they should just let me sit down with some of these folks. I'd get their heads on straight."

"Perhaps you should suggest that to the doctors," Denny muttered as he aimed his flashlight farther down the hall. "Leave him be, Tommy. We've got a lot of halls to patrol."

Suddenly, Denny heard a painful groan. When he turned around, Tommy was curled up in a ball on the floor, and a young woman, no . . . a girl, dressed entirely in black, was standing over him. Denny didn't know whether to run for help or give the attacker a hug.

"I took a chance," the girl said. "I'm hoping you're the smart one."

"Yes, that would be right," Denny said.

"Tell me about Felix Jigsaw," she said.

"The Jigsaw Puzzle King?" Denny said.

"The what?"

"The Jigsaw Puzzle King," the guard said. "Don't you read the papers?"

"I've been a little busy being twelve years old," she replied.

"Felix Jigsaw was a brilliant scientist, or so I read. He specialized in tectonic plate theory, you know, the movement of continents. He was famous for his work on the Pangaea theory."

"Huh?"

"He dedicated his life to proving that all the continents had once been one big island, which broke into pieces. He was also famous for being a star in the competitive jigsaw puzzle circuit. Some called him the Tiger Woods of jigsaw puzzles, but if you ask me it was the puzzles that drove him crazy. The moment he was locked up in here it was all puzzles, day and night. He was obsessed. Still, he wasn't a criminal so they couldn't keep him. Someone signed him out and that was the last I saw of him."

"They let him go? Does that mean he was cured?"

Denny chuckled. "You don't get cured of what Jigsaw has. No, someone agreed to look after him."

"Who?"

Denny led her to a dark office. He tapped a few keys into a computer and pulled up a file. Scrolling down, he found what he was looking for. "Here, this is who signed him out. A guy named Simon. Can't tell you if that's his first or last name."

The Hyena frowned.

"Why are you so curious about this nutcase?" Denny asked.

"I work for him," she said.

13

Jackson was curled in a ball on the floor of the rocket breathing in and out into a paper sack. Ms. Holiday knelt over him, rubbing his back and squeezing his hand to comfort him. "Just relax, Jackson."

"Relax?" Jackson cried through his hyperventilation. "I'm in outer space. I signed up to be a spy, not an astronaut."

"How pathetic," Heathcliff said.

"Yeah, maybe we should call *him* Wheezer," Matilda added.

"Be nice," Ms. Holiday scolded.

"Jackson, this is the most efficient method of transport," Mr. Brand explained.

"He's right," Duncan said. "Instead of flying across the globe for hours, the School Bus flies up into the stratosphere and then back down where we want. It shortens a flight from several hours to no more than thirty minutes, allowing us to get back to school before the end of the day."

"If the new guy's nervous breakdown is over, perhaps we should get into our gear," Ruby said.

The children snatched the packs from the front of the rocket. Jackson found the one with his name on it, opened it up, and pulled out a heavy wool shirt and pants, a thick lamb's wool coat, and a small cotton hat.

"Uh, this is just a bunch of clothing. Where's the secret agent stuff? Where's the exploding bow tie and the camera pen?"

"Everyone's pack is assembled for their specific needs," Ms. Holiday said.

"How am I going to do spy stuff with all this?" he cried.

"You're not," Brand said. "You're observing on this mission."

"What?" Jackson cried. He felt the rocket turn back toward Earth, and his belly did a flip. "I've been training for weeks. I'm ready."

"How many people think Braceface is ready?" Ruby said to the team. None of them raised their hands.

"The desert is sparsely inhabited, and we don't expect you'll meet many locals," Ms. Holiday said. "But if you do, they will probably be of two types—sheepherders or armed tribal fighters who won't take kindly to trespassers. Do your best to avoid them."

"Once you get into the city, you'll pose as street kids peddling wares in the market," Agent Brand said. "Each of you has been briefed on your specific tasks once you've found Dr. Badawi's lab."

"Briefed? I wasn't briefed." Jackson said.

Brand ignored him. "Ms. Holiday, what can you tell us about the good Dr. Badawi?"

"Dr. Badawi is married to American diplomat Omar Badawi, who is currently the United States ambassador to Egypt. Her lab is in a bustling tourist corridor of Cairo called the Spice Market. To get there, you're going to travel through the Sahara desert. The sun will be brutal, and the clothes I packed you will protect you from burning, but will also keep you warm at night, in case this mission takes longer than expected. Pufferfish, Wheezer, you'll find extra sets of clothing in your packs, as we discussed."

"Got 'em," Wheezer said.

"Flinch, I've packed a dozen marshmallow pies and a case of juice boxes, if you need them."

Flinch licked his lips. "You are a beautiful person, Ms. Holiday."

"What's this?" Matilda said as she pulled a chocolate chip cookie out of her pack.

"Oh, that's from me," Ms. Holiday said. "I wanted to give you all a good-luck treat."

The herd stared at her in disbelief—they clearly weren't used to being coddled, and they weren't sure they liked it. But then they shrugged and started dressing for their mission. Jackson found his sheepherder outfit very scratchy. "You can spend ten billion on my superbraces, but you don't have a couple bucks for fabric softener?" he muttered.

Once everyone was dressed, they returned to their seats and locked their safety belts. Jackson had been on planes, and always found putting on his seat belt to be tedious and silly. But the descent in the School Bus changed his mind forever. It was even more terrifying than the takeoff, like a free fall right into the ground, until the lunch lady leveled the ship off above the desert floor.

"We're over the drop," the pilot grunted.

"The drop?" Jackson asked.

Suddenly, Brand was out of his seat and opening the hatch at the front of the jet. The other kids followed him, each snatching a parachute from a pile stacked nearby.

"No one told me we were jumping out of a rocket!" Jackson shouted. "I've never done this before."

"It's pretty easy," Matilda said. "All you have to do is fall."

A moment later, she jumped out and was gone.

Heathcliff was next, then Ruby.

"Your ride will be along soon," Brand shouted over the wind.

Ruby nodded as she jumped outside.

Flinch raced to the front, snatched a pack, and leaped outside without even putting it on his back.

Jackson screamed, sure he had just witnessed the boy's last moments alive, but Duncan assured him Flinch was OK. "He does that every time. He's a bit of an adrenaline junkie."

"He's a bit of a lunatic," Jackson mumbled.

"You and I are going together," Duncan said. He ran his hands up and down Jackson's back. When Jackson craned his neck he noticed a sticky film trail where the boy's hands had been. Then Duncan hugged him from behind. The two boys were stuck tight.

Ms. Holiday helped the chubby spy into his parachute while Jackson squirmed for his freedom.

"You realize we are all minors," Jackson said. "You're letting six children jump out of a plane, into the desert, in a foreign country, alone."

"You'll be fine," Duncan said to Jackson. "I'll keep you safe."

"You ate fourteen glue sticks in art class once. I don't think you're the best one to protect me," Jackson said.

"Find the doctor and bring her back," Brand said. "Jackson, Ruby is your team leader and unless she directs you otherwise, your job on this mission is to observe."

"Wait, maybe I *should* stay in the rocket!" Jackson cried, but he never finished his sentence. Duncan dragged him through the open door. Jackson's screams were drowned out by the wind, but he could still hear them inside his head as the ground raced toward them.

"Isn't it beautiful up here?" Duncan shouted.

Jackson just kept on screaming. Eventually, he felt Duncan pull a cord. There was a loud *pop*, and then an incredible flapping sound as the parachute unfolded above them. When it unfurled, the boys were jerked roughly upward. Then they began to slowly descend.

"I love this part," Duncan said. "It's so peaceful."

The boys landed on the edge of a dune and tumbled face-first into the sand. As they rolled, the parachute wrapped around them so that neither could move a muscle. Jackson now knew what it must feel like to be a burrito.

As they tried to untangle themselves, the rest of the team sprang into action. They buried their parachutes, while Ruby used binoculars to scan the valley. "Here comes our ride," she said.

Jackson turned his head in the direction Ruby was looking. He saw a lone figure walking toward them with six camels in tow.

"You've got to be kidding," Jackson said. "We're riding camels to Cairo?"

"Aaagha bezzzeter chuck," Flinch said.

"Huh?"

The hyperactive boy turned the knob on his body harness. "I said 'camels rule, bro!'"

Ruby ignored the chatter. "Let's move, people."

"Uh, we're kind of stuck!" Jackson cried from inside the parachute burrito.

"No worries," Duncan said. "Laser watch activate."

Duncan's wristwatch opened and a tiny laser cannon poked out. It targeted the straps of the parachute, and moments later the two boys were free.

"I didn't get a laser watch," Jackson grumbled.

"I know," Duncan said with a smile. "It's only for the good agents."

With the camel salesman's help, Jackson and the others mounted their animals. Once they were safely aboard, the old man smacked Jackson's camel on the rump, sending him racing into the desert. It turned out riding a camel was like being on a smelly inner tube trapped in white-water rapids. He fell off the furry monster a dozen times, and each time, the camel reached down and bit him. His teammates just laughed.

Worse, the sun was broiling. The disguises the librarian had given them protected against its vicious rays, but felt heavy in the heat. Jackson complained, and the others ignored him.

They had been traveling for a couple of hours when Ruby

called for them to take a break. She pointed out a rocky outcropping and led the rest of the team toward it.

Jackson attempted to dismount, but his camel bucked and kicked, sending him sprawling onto the ground. He couldn't be sure, but it seemed as if the beast was giggling at him, just like the rest of his team. He picked himself up and pulled his pack off the camel's back. Inside he found several bottles of water and Ms. Holiday's cookie. He decided he needed a treat and took a bite. The cookie was as hard as stone and tasted like vinegar. He wrapped it back up and put it in his shirt pocket. Clearly, Ms. Holiday could not bake.

"How long do you think we'll be here?" Jackson asked Ruby. She ignored him. She took a school organizer out of her pack and opened it up. Where folders and rulers should have been, there was a computer monitor and keyboard, as well as a tiny satellite dish spinning in circles.

"Probably a half hour," Duncan said. "Ruby likes to get topographic maps and weather before we get into the heat of the mission. It will take a while to link to Benjamin."

Jackson laid back and closed his eyes. "I think I'll take a nap, then."

"Do what you want, but don't expect a bedtime story from me," Wheezer said.

• • •

When Jackson awoke, the sun was in his eyes, his mouth was dry, and he had a knife across his throat. He looked up and saw the owner of the blade—a dark-skinned man with a long beard and stringy black hair. He wore loose, flowing white pants and a green shirt and had a leather belt lined with shotgun shells. He barked something in a language Jackson didn't understand. Out of the corner of his eye, Jackson saw more men just like him, all brandishing ugly swords and shouting threats. He didn't have to be multilingual to know they were angry.

"Try to relax," Ruby said to him. "No sudden movements. These are local tribal fighters and we've stumbled onto their land."

"How do you know that?" Jackson said as he craned his neck to see her. She was standing behind him. A group of men had their swords aimed at her heart.

"Call it a hunch," Ruby said.

"Where are the others?" Jackson asked.

"I sent them ahead to scout the highway into Cairo. They won't be back for an hour," the girl replied.

"So we're here alone?" Jackson cried. The man holding the sword shouted at him angrily and pressed his blade closer to his Adam's apple.

"You remember me telling you to relax, right?" Ruby said.

"So what are we going to do?" Jackson said more quietly.

"Well, we have two choices. We can die, which is what these

guys want us to do, or we can fight back and die a little later. You choose."

"Don't you have some spy gadget or gizmo?" Jackson asked. "What about your upgrades?"

"Mine are inside my body, doofus. My allergies make me highly sensitive to danger—almost bordering on psychic. For instance, my tongue is swollen because I'm allergic to angry threats. My eyes are itchy because I'm allergic to large groups of people with swords. My ears feel clogged because I'm allergic to answering dumb questions. My ability is not going to help us much here. Why don't you use your upgrades?"

"I don't know how to use them yet," Jackson said. "All I know is that I can use my braces to catch a flying car and force-feed a dog. I haven't had a single lesson on what they can do."

"I told Brand you weren't ready," Ruby said. "I wish Gluestick was here. He's a technology guy, but I'll do my best to explain. Your braces are made from millions of tiny robots called nanobytes. They are linked to your brain so you have control over them. If you want them to react, all you have to do is to think it."

Jackson concentrated and he could feel the wires swirling around in his mouth, and in a flash a crudely shaped fist rocketed out of his mouth and caught the warrior leader under the chin. He dropped his saber and fell backward into the sand.

The other warriors raised their swords in the air and screamed in fury. Six strands shot out of Jackson's mouth, all with swords at the ends. The fighters slashed with their weapons, but Jackson's braces blocked each attack. Jackson felt like he had six musketeers in his mouth. Metal crashed into metal and sparks flew everywhere. Finally, Jackson managed to disarm the entire gang, and they ran off in fear.

"Did you see that?" Jackson cried as his braces retracted into his mouth. "I rule!"

"That was hardly worth the self-congratulations," Ruby said.

"What? Was I the only one standing here? Those guys were going to kill us. You're lucky I was here to save your itchy behind."

"Let's just get something straight!" Ruby shouted. "We don't need your help in any way, shape, or form. Each one of us is an expertly trained fighting machine. We all know how to paralyze a man with just a pinch. You're on this team despite the fact that all of us voted against you. Our votes used to mean something . . . anyway, just because we're stuck with you doesn't mean we're ever going to be buddies or grateful to you for anything. You're a bully—"

"What?" Jackson cried.

"A bully!" Ruby shouted even louder. "So you fought off a

few bad guys. If you think I would do the same for you, then you're dumber than you look. You're on your own, and if you think you can intimidate us with a wedgie or a headlock, you've got another think coming."

"So I guess you're not going to thank me?" Jackson said.

An hour later, Matilda floated to the ground with Duncan in her arms. In the distance they spotted a streak of dust heading in their direction. When it stopped just six inches away, Jackson realized it was Flinch with Heathcliff on his back.

"Oh, I always miss the fun," Matilda complained when she saw the piles of weapons.

"Some fighters decided to mess with Jackson Jones!" Jackson crowed. "They learned the hard way how tough I am."

Ruby turned away. "Let's get going. We've got several more miles before we get to the lab, and who knows how many more of these fighters are lurking about."

The others were soon climbing aboard their camels.

Jackson was annoyed. "What? No pat on the back? No good job, Jackson? Where's the gratitude?"

The others ignored him and trotted off.

Cairo was a fascinating place. Skyscrapers rose high into the air next to ancient stone buildings. Taxis and sports cars shared the roads with camels and donkeys. Men in suits rushed off to work while farmers pushed carts of exotic fruits and vegetables to market.

A policeman yelled at the NERDS team. "He wants us off the main road," Heathcliff told the others after searching through an Arabic-to-English dictionary. "He called us filthy gypsies."

"He's not very nice," Duncan said.

Ruby steered her camel down a side street, and the team followed. She led them down several crowded alleyways. Children played while tourists gawked at the buildings and snapped endless photographs. Women carried baskets of laundry on their heads as tiny European cars struggled to get past.

"Badawi's lab is around this corner," Ruby said as she hopped off her camel. The others followed her lead. "Intelligence says she has several armed guards, and it would be best if we can avoid them. Wheezer, you and I will need to get changed. Flinch, Gluestick, and Choppers, circle the building and try to find where those guards are positioned."

The three boys ran off.

"What about me?" Jackson said.

"You can turn around," Matilda said. After several moments the girls tapped Jackson on the shoulder. He spun around and found them wearing Girl Scout uniforms.

"Again, I missed the briefing," Jackson said. "What is going on?"

Before they could explain, the boys returned. "There's two guards on a fire escape on the west side of the building," Heathcliff said.

"There's two at the front door," Duncan added.

"Nothing on the roof," Flinch said as he opened three juice boxes and sipped them all at the same time. It wasn't long before he was shaking and giggling from the sugar.

"OK, we're going to distract as many guards as possible," Matilda said.

"How do you plan on doing that?" Jackson asked.

Matilda dug into her pack and pulled out several boxes of cookies. "With these."

"No one can resist Girl Scout cookies," Ruby said. "As for the rest of you, it looks like the roof is the safest way inside."

"What about me?" Jackson asked.

"You've got the most important job ever."

Jackson's eyes popped open. "Really? What?"

"You get to guard the camels."

Jackson scowled. "I'm not used to sitting on the bench."

Ruby pointed an angry finger at him. "Then you better get used to it. You're here to observe."

"Forget it!" Jackson snapped.

"Listen, he can go with us," Duncan said.

"With us?" Flinch and Heathcliff cried.

"I'll take responsibility for him," Duncan insisted.

"If he screws up, it's on you, Gluestick," Ruby said.

"No worries," Duncan said. Heathcliff shot him a murderous look, but he kept his mouth closed.

"All right, let's go kidnap us a scientist," Flinch said as he clapped his hands.

The girls headed for the front door, while the boys circled around the back of the building.

"So, how do we get up to the roof?" Jackson asked, eyeing the building. It was easily ten feet tall. "There's no rope in my pack."

"Like this," Flinch said as he grabbed Heathcliff and tossed him high into the air. Jackson watched as the bucktoothed spy landed nimbly on the roof of the building.

"No way you are doing that to me!" Jackson said. It looked more terrifying than the rocket.

"It's really safe," Duncan said, just before he was tossed as well.

"He's right," Flinch said. "I've only crippled three people. That's a very good percentage."

"Now, let's talk about this," Jackson said, but a moment later the boy's hands hefted him off the ground and flung him high into the sky. Flinch's toss was perfect and Jackson came down on the roof like a feather. A barfing, crying feather—but a feather nonetheless.

Flinch landed beside him, grinning from ear to ear. "Fun, huh?"

The other boys pulled off their desert clothes, revealing black bodysuits covered in zippered pockets. Duncan took out a pair of goggles, slipped them over his eyes, and looked down at the roof.

"The girls are having some luck. The guards are gone from the fire escape. I'm detecting two people in a lab on the eighth floor. Braceface, want to take a look?" He handed the goggles to Jackson.

"Stop calling me Braceface," Jackson said as he slipped them on and looked down. He could see red silhouettes shaped like people rushing about inside the building. The X-ray sensor goggles were amazing. "So, how do we get inside?"

Heathcliff gestured to a fire escape door on the roof. "Duh!"

Jackson also pointed to the huge lock on the door. "Double duh!"

"I'll take care of that," Flinch said, turning the dial on his harness. He ripped the door off its hinges and tossed it aside like a scrap of paper. "Ta-da!"

The four boys hurried though the door and down the stairs.

"She's two floors down," Duncan said.

"Pufferfish, how's the cookie sale going?" Heathcliff said.

"Very well," a voice echoed inside Jackson's head. He recognized it as Ruby's.

"I heard her in my head," Jackson cried.

"Communications are linked through the chip inside your nose," Duncan explained. "If you need to talk to one of us, just focus on our faces in your mind. The chip does the rest."

The boys continued down to the eighth floor of the building and slipped into the hallway. Before they had a chance to regroup, a guard appeared. Luckily, the team leaped into an empty room before he spotted them.

"Flinch, you and Gluestick go after Dr. Badawi," said Heathcliff. "I'll stay here and babysit the dead weight."

The two boys raced into the hallway and vanished, leaving Jackson and Heathcliff alone. They sat in silence for a long time until Jackson's curiosity got the best of him.

"Why do you hate me so much?"

"As if you have to ask," Heathcliff said.

"Actually, I do have to ask. That's why I'm asking."

Heathcliff let out an impatient sigh. "NERDS is an organization like no other, because its members are chosen for their skills and abilities."

"And you don't think I have skills and abilities," Jackson said. "I'm a star athlete."

"So what? Who cares if you can throw a football? The world is not saved by touchdowns—it's saved by ideas. This organization has always had an elite membership. Our members go on to be diplomats, scientists, and inventors—very few of them spend as much time on their hair as you do. Your very existence here is a slap in the face to every person who has ever risked his or her life as a member of this team."

Jackson felt his face flush. "Brand seems to think I have potential."

"Agent Brand sees himself in you," Heathcliff replied. "But like you, he could never have been one of us. We're the guys they call when people like Brand can't get the job done."

Jackson looked away. He didn't want Heathcliff to see that his words had hurt him.

"It's all clear," Flinch said in Jackson's head. "I've got the guard under control and Gluestick is on his way to pick up the package."

"Good," Heathcliff said.

"Sit tight and we'll be back to get you," Flinch replied.

"Choppers to the School Bus," Heathcliff said out loud. A moment later, Jackson heard the lunch lady's gravelly voice.

"School Bus is here."

"Gluestick is retrieving the package. Request extraction," Heathcliff said.

"On our way, kid," the pilot replied.

While this conversation was taking place, Jackson heard something in the distance. It sounded like a heavy machine coming in their direction, loud and fast. He stood up and went to the window. As he peeked outside, a helicopter flew directly over the building.

"Uh, any idea who that is?" Jackson said. He studied the helicopter. It didn't have any markings on it at all.

Heathcliff rushed to the window and craned his neck to see the new arrival. "I don't have a clue. Team, we have an unidentified helicopter in the area. Gluestick, do you have the doctor?"

There was a brief pause and then Duncan's voice could be heard. "Not yet. Whoever it is, I recommend you engage. It will give us more time to acquire the target."

"Negative," Ruby said. "Work faster."

Jackson watched the helicopter land on the roof of the lab. A moment later, he heard heavy feet rushing down the stairs the boys had just taken. Jackson and Heathcliff raced over to the doorway and peered out into the hall. A dozen heavily armed men were running down the stairs from the roof. Among them was a young girl, no older than Jackson, with platinum blonde hair. She said something to the men and they raced down the hallway past the boys' hiding spot.

"They're in the building," Jackson said. "You've got to warn the others."

"I can see that!" Heathcliff snapped. "Gluestick, can you hear me? Wheezer? Choppers? Flinch? Can anyone hear me? Abort the mission!"

"It's too late," Flinch said. He sounded nervous in Jackson's head. "They're storming into the doctor's lab now. Gluestick is in there. Where did these guys come from?"

Heathcliff frowned.

"We have to save them," Jackson said.

"Absolutely not. You're here to observe and we are outmatched."

But Jackson was already running down the hallway after the armed men. Heathcliff may not have had any faith in him, but he'd show that jerk. He was Jackson Jones, and Jackson Jones did not sit on the bench.

14

Dr. Jigsaw said it would be simple. All the Hyena had to do was to storm the lab, kidnap the scientist, and go, but did it turn out like that? No! Nothing was ever simple when you worked for a crazy person.

It was, of course, her own fault, because she should have known better. She should have quit the moment she saw Dr. Lunich die in a fiery inferno. She should have quit when she saw what Jigsaw's continent-moving machine could do. She should have quit when she discovered Jigsaw had been in a mental hospital for a nervous breakdown, but she realized that if she quit every job because the boss was a lunatic, she would never work again. But now he had gone too far. He had saddled her with a team of morons who were heavy on weaponry and short on attention span.

As goons went, they were really quite useless. If she hadn't reminded them to show up at the airport at a certain time, they would never have gotten on the plane. If she hadn't personally made wake-up calls to get them out of bed on time, they would have slept through the mission. And meals—oh, the meals on the mission were the worst. Picking a restaurant to eat in took hours and usually ended in an angry squabble. One wanted fried chicken; another had to have chili. One was on a special no-carb diet. The other was allergic to wheat and eggs. There was no making them happy.

But the morning of the actual kidnapping, the Hyena thought she had whipped them all into shape. Everyone was showered, dressed, and ready when the helicopter landed. Everyone had had breakfast. No one had to go to the bathroom at the last minute, and best of all, they had remembered to bring their weapons with them.

When they landed on the roof of the doctor's building, she led the goons down to the lab, where they found a locked door. There are many ways through a locked door. One can pick the lock. One can slide a credit card along the crack where the door and the frame meet. One can use a crowbar and pry a door open. One can even knock. But the goons had another method—kicking a door off its hinges. They dashed in, fully prepared to snatch a screaming scientist, when the Hyena saw something she didn't expect. Standing with mouth agape was a chubby African American boy dressed in a black jumpsuit. He was clutching Dr. Badawi's arm as if he were preparing to drag her away.

"Who are you?" the Hyena demanded.

The chubby boy thrust out his hands and a thick, yellow substance squirted out of the tips of his fingers. It landed all over her boots and the floor.

"Hey! Watch the boots. They're new!" she cried, but the boy was already on the move. He hoisted the tiny scientist onto his shoulder like a sack of apples and then did something the Hyena would not have thought possible if she hadn't seen it herself. He ran up the side of the room and onto the ceiling like a human fly. Each step left more of the gooey yellow glop behind. Soon he and the scientist were racing across the ceiling and out of the lab.

Once the Hyena came to her senses, she attempted to chase after them, but her feet held fast to the floor. In fact, she couldn't move a pinky toe in any direction. The stuff the fat kid had squirted on her was some kind of super-powerful glue.

"What should we do?" one of the goons asked.

"Um, you could go after them," the Hyena suggested sarcastically.

A moment later the goons were piling out through the lab door and she was struggling with her boots.

"Not again!" the Hyena muttered as she reached down to

unzip them. She slid her feet out and gave her boots a strong tug. It did no good. The weird kid's glue was like concrete. Another six hundred dollars down the drain!

Furious, she turned and raced barefoot into the hallway. The kid and the scientist were nowhere in sight, but another boy had appeared in front of her. This one, unlike the sticky weirdo, was cute, though he had a set of braces that appeared to be made from battleship scraps.

"Give up," the boy said. "We've got her now."

The Hyena frowned. "My boss doesn't pay for me to give up."

She was about to push past him when something crazy happened. The boy opened his mouth and strands of his braces sprang out, formed a giant hand, and latched onto her arm. She tried to pull away, but the braces wouldn't allow it.

"Let me go, you carnival reject," she demanded.

"Not until you call off your goons," the boy said.

The Hyena had had enough. Cute or not, this boy was in her way. Her arms weren't free, but her feet were. She aimed a kick at the boy's chin. His weird braces loosened their grip, and the Hyena slipped out and raced for the stairs.

Unfortunately, when she got downstairs to the street, she found her so-called crack team of mercenaries getting their butts handed to them by another eleven-year-old boy. He was dressed in a weird harness and was tossing the goons around like rag dolls. He was scrawny, but had unbelievable strength. She watched him punch one of her goons, a man three times his size, sending him tumbling thirty yards down the street. But he wasn't the only obstacle. Flying above them was an Asian girl—were those inhalers in her hands?—who kept buzzing by the goons, distracting them. Then there was another boy with bright red hair and the biggest set of front teeth she had ever seen on a human being. She couldn't be sure how he was doing it, but he had somehow convinced half of her team to turn on itself. Soon the goons were in the midst of an all-out brawl. The Hyena raced into the melee, dodging flying fists and angry elbows. The sticky boy and the scientist were weaving through the crowd ahead of the Hyena, but her agility and speed would allow her to catch up to them fast. She was within hands' reach of her prey when the boy with braces materialized again.

"You've got my scientist," the Hyena said to him.

"Sorry, finders keepers," he replied as four long metallic arms crept out of his mouth, planted themselves on the ground, and lifted him up like a spider.

"OK, that's cool in a very disgusting kind of way, but I recommend you move," she said.

"Can't do that," the boy said.

"Your mistake," she said as she leaped into the air. She planted her hands on his shoulders and used him as a springboard to flip herself over his body. She kicked him in the back of the head in the process. He fell hard on his face, but she didn't stick around to see if he was hurt. Glue boy and the scientist were climbing aboard a camel and racing off down a back alley. She'd never catch them on foot. Spotting another camel nearby, she climbed into its saddle, took the reins, and dug her heels into the animal's ribs. It roared and took off like a rocket.

The Hyena had ridden many horses in her day; equestrian talents were a major plus in the world of beauty pageants. But a

camel is only similar to a horse in that it has hair and four legs. Riding a horse is like floating on smooth waves. Riding a camel is like riding a barrel over a waterfall: bouncy, uncomfortable, and, factoring in camel saliva, very wet. Still, the Hyena would rather face camel spit than go back to Jigsaw empty-handed. She was not going into the fire pit like Dr. Lunich!

They raced down back alleys, weaving through hidden neighborhoods and causing panicked people to leap out of their way. An old woman tossed a pail of brown water out of her window right on the Hyena's head. A man dragged a cart

with a broken wheel across her path. After much shouting, she got around him and continued her pursuit. Her target made a left turn onto a long stretch of lonely road that crossed over an empty riverbed. The Hyena dug her heels into the camel again and soon the distance between her and the sticky boy had shortened.

She was seconds away when the odd boy with the mechanical mouth came stomping past her. He sidled up to the chubby boy, then a fifth limb crept out of his mouth and pulled Dr. Badawi away from Glueboy. Glueboy shouted angrily at Metalmouth, but in the process, he fell off his camel and tumbled end over end down the embankment to the dry riverbed below. Metalmouth, however, just kept running. If he noticed that his companion had taken a nosedive into the dust, he didn't seem concerned.

The Hyena raced after him, but his machine legs outpaced the camel two steps to one, and in no time he was out of the city proper and into the hot, brutal desert. As he slipped farther and farther away, the Hyena began to feel Dr. Jigsaw's trap door sliding out from under her. She was nearly resigned to a fiery death when a miracle occurred. As she chased the boy up a sandy embankment, she saw an army of men on horseback approach. Each was brandishing a huge sword and screaming angry threats into the air. The men surrounded them all.

The leader of the militia pointed his sword at the boy's neck and shouted angrily.

"Friends of yours?" the Hyena asked him.

"A few of them had me surrounded this afternoon. I think he's still angry about the beating I gave him," the boy replied.

"You've disgraced his manhood," she said. "You should apologize before he chops off your head."

"I don't speak Arabic," the boy said.

"I do," the Hyena said. "Give me the doctor and I'll get you out of this."

The boy frowned, but a moment later his tentacles were easing the poor doctor onto the back of the Hyena's camel.

"Thanks," she said, as she turned the camel in the opposite direction.

"Hey! I thought you were going to help me!"

"Yeah, about that. I don't really speak their language. But good luck," she said, then clomped off into the night. She heard an enormous roar from the crowd and the sound of swords clanging.

15

"I'm sensing that you're angry," Jackson said as Agent Brand paced back and forth. The spy said nothing. Neither did the scientists hovering about in the Playground. Jackson had never heard headquarters so still.

"I think it's clear that he's not cut out for this," Ruby said before Brand could answer.

Flinch turned the knob on his harness. "He really blew it."

Jackson was livid. "What did you think—I was going to be some superspy right out of the box?"

"What I thought was you could follow simple orders!" Agent Brand shouted. His words were so loud, Ms. Holiday yelped. "I told you to observe, not get involved."

"The team needed my help!"

"That's ridiculous," Heathcliff muttered. "We had the situation under control. We've faced bigger problems than a dozen armed goons."

"Heathcliff is right," Brand said. "Your teammates are more than capable. You, however, are not. You are responsible for Dr. Badawi's kidnapping."

"Technically, she was supposed to get kidnapped," Jackson said.

"By us!" Heathcliff cried.

"Plus, you let the enemy know that we are onto them. We've lost the element of surprise," Matilda said.

Jackson shook his head. Badawi would have been snatched by the girl and her goons whether he had tried to help or not. Wasn't anyone going to point out that little nugget of information?

"We should wipe his mind and send him back to class," Heathcliff said.

Jackson turned to Duncan. The boy had shown signs of sympathy toward him. Maybe he'd speak up, but Duncan was silently rubbing a bruise on his behind and scowling angrily.

"I agree," Flinch said.

"So do I," Ruby said. "As team leader, I'm calling for a vote. All those in favor of expelling Joe Quarterback here, say—"

Brand slammed his hand on the table. Somewhere a guinea pig camera squeaked in fright. "You're as stubborn as Jackson!" Brand cried.

Ruby started furiously scratching her legs.

"What's wrong with you?" Brand asked the girl.

"She's allergic to criticism," Matilda said.

Brand groaned. "What has happened to my career! I used to drive an Aston Martin. I used to play high-stakes card games for the fate of the world. I used to date beautiful women."

"Gross!" Flinch said.

"Now look at me." The spy threw up his hands in exasperation and stormed out of the room.

Ms. Holiday brushed the wrinkles from her skirt and stepped forward. "Pufferfish, I'm very disappointed."

"What did I do?"

"That man is one of the greatest secret agents this country has ever seen," Ms. Holiday said. "He lost part of his leg trying to save the world. The Powers That Be have put him in charge of this group. Perhaps they know something about him that you don't?"

"I don't need to know anything about him," Ruby muttered.

"I want all of you to get to work now with Benjamin. Load any information about this mysterious girl you encountered and try to build a three-dimensional model of her so we can search for face matches," Ms. Holiday said.

"What about me?" Jackson asked.

"I said *all* of you, Braceface," the librarian replied.

"So you're not firing me?"

"Not today."

"Why not?" Heathcliff begged.

Ms. Holiday flashed Jackson a sympathetic smile as she walked off in the direction of Agent Brand.

"You're running out of chances," Heathcliff said to Jackson.

"It's just a matter of time before you're gone," Matilda added.

Jackson was about to argue, but something dawned on him. "Time! What time is it?"

Duncan looked at his watch. Apparently it did more than shoot lasers. "It's four thirty."

"Four thirty!" Jackson cried. "I'm late for detention!" Dehaven was going to kill him!

Jackson raced toward the secret entrance that led him out of the lockers. When he was back in the school hallway, he took off at a sprint toward the detention room. He rounded the corner and threw the door open, but the room was empty. There wasn't a soul waiting inside, only a note written on the chalkboard. It read:

YOU MESSED WITH THE BULL, JACKSON. NOW IT'S TIME FOR THE HORNS.

END TRANSMISSION.

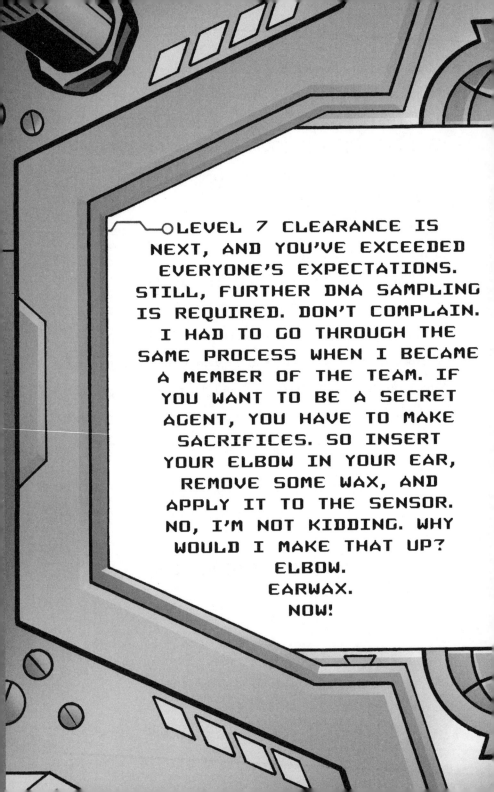

LEVEL 7 CLEARANCE IS NEXT, AND YOU'VE EXCEEDED EVERYONE'S EXPECTATIONS. STILL, FURTHER DNA SAMPLING IS REQUIRED. DON'T COMPLAIN. I HAD TO GO THROUGH THE SAME PROCESS WHEN I BECAME A MEMBER OF THE TEAM. IF YOU WANT TO BE A SECRET AGENT, YOU HAVE TO MAKE SACRIFICES. SO INSERT YOUR ELBOW IN YOUR EAR, REMOVE SOME WAX, AND APPLY IT TO THE SENSOR. NO, I'M NOT KIDDING. WHY WOULD I MAKE THAT UP? ELBOW. EARWAX. NOW!

LEVEL 7
ACCESS GRANTED

BEGIN TRANSMISSION:

BY THE WAY—
THAT WAS THE FUNNIEST
THING I'VE EVER SEEN.
YOU LOOKED RIDICULOUS.

16

THE FOLLOWING ARE RECORDED TRANSCRIPTS OF CALLS MADE FROM THE HYENA'S DIGITAL PHONE TO UNKNOWN PERSONS.

September 30, 13:05

Unknown: Hello.

Hyena: Hey, my name is the Hyena. I'm a professional assassin and I was wondering if you guys need anyone killed over there. I do a lot of freelance work.

Unknown: Uh, what did you say your name was?

Hyena: The Hyena.

Unknown: Yeah, well, thanks for your call, but we do our killing in-house.

Hyena: Well, could I at least send my résumé?

You never know when problems might spring up.

Unknown: How old are you?

Hyena: I'm twelve . . . almost thirteen.

<Connection is lost>

Hyena: Hello? Hello?

September 30, 13:20

Unknown: Secret Lair. How can I help you?

Hyena: I was wondering if you're hiring contract killers.

Unknown: Hmmm, I don't think so. I know we've got plenty of positions open for goons.

Hyena: No thanks.

September 30, 13:28

Unknown: Fortress of Doom. How can I direct your call?

Hyena: Yes, I saw your ad for the assassin job.

Unknown: Let me transfer you to our human resources department.

<CLICK>

Unknown HR: Human Resources.

Hyena: Yes, I was calling in regard to the ad I saw on Craigslist for the assassin job.

Unknown HR: Yes, I'm afraid we filled that position.

Hyena: Fudge.

Unknown HR: But the boss just went on a killing spree yesterday and a dozen henchmen were cut in half by our giant saw.

Hyena: Henchman, huh? What's the costume?

Unknown HR: Bumblebee.

Hyena: (Sighs) How bad is it?

Unknown HR: (Whispering) Between you and me, it's horrible. The suit is yellow and black and makes you look fat. Black tights, black turtleneck, goofy hat with bouncy antennas, but the worst part is the stinger on the bum. The boss has a thing about hives. Calls himself the Yellow Jacket. Looks like a complete moron . . .

<LOUD SOUND>

Unknown HR: Hey! Let go of me!

Hyena: What's going on?

Unknown HR: No, I won't go. No! Oh, help me. They're taking me to the saw!

<Connection is lost>

September 30, 13:30

Unknown:	Domino's Pizza.
Hyena:	Yeah, how far north do you deliver?
Unknown:	How far north are you?
Hyena:	By the pole.
Unknown:	What pole?
Hyena:	The North one.

<Connection is lost>

| Hyena: | I hate this crummy job. |

17

When Jackson arrived home, he weighed his options. Should he tell his father about his secret life? Or keep silent? He had promised never to reveal the existence of NERDS, but he began to wonder if it was a promise he could keep.

As he opened his front door, he made a decision. "Dad! I have something important to tell you," he shouted as he entered the house and walked down the hall. In the dining room, he saw something that shocked him to the core. Mr. Dehaven was sipping a cup of coffee. Jackson's father was sitting across from him. Butch was in a chair too. Jackson wasn't sure which of the three had the more disapproving look.

"Good evening, Mr. Jones," Mr. Dehaven said. "You missed our appointment today, so I took the liberty of making a personal visit to find out why. Your father and I have had a chat about your grades and attitude."

"Have a seat, buster," Jackson's father said.

The lecture that followed this request was peppered with words like "disappointed," "astonished," "surprised," "furious," and "flabbergasted." All the while, Dehaven sat idly by with an amused smile.

"Jackson, do you have an explanation for all of this?" his father demanded.

Jackson felt like standing up and shouting, "Yes! I have an explanation. I'm a secret agent and all day long I work with a team that saves the world from bad guys. We have a rocket and laser watches and a nose walkie-talkie and guinea pig cameras, and it is eating up every moment of my life!"

But he didn't. Instead he dropped his head and apologized.

"Well, you can forget the marching band and all the other extracurricular activities you're involved with. Plus, no TV or video games until your grades are back up to snuff."

"Mr. Jones, I think those are all very good starts, but I'm afraid I have to send a clear message, not only to Jackson but to the other troublemaking students at Nathan Hale. I'm going to have to suspend Jackson for three days."

Jackson's father took a deep breath and pointed upward. "To your room!"

As Jackson backed out of the room, he saw Dehaven make little bull horns on the sides of his head.

Jackson climbed the stairs to his room and closed the door behind him. He flopped down on his bed and stared up at the ceiling. He could still feel sand between his toes and was sure there was a pound of it trapped in his underwear.

Just then, his bedroom door opened. Chaz poked his head inside. "What's all the commotion, Nerdbot?"

"I got suspended from school," Jackson explained.

"Duh! People on the next block know that," his brother said. "The way dad was shouting, I wasn't sure you were going to survive. Does this have something to do with your new friends?"

Jackson nodded.

"How could you hang out with those losers?" Chaz's face curled up like he had just smelled something foul.

"No one else wanted me," Jackson said. The truth was sour in his mouth.

"I'd rather be alone than hang out with those dorks," Chaz said. "Tell Dad I went to practice."

A moment later, he was gone.

Jackson looked over at the desk in his room. There he saw a picture of his father, Chaz, and him. His mother had taken it at a Washington Redskins game. The three of them had their arms around each other's shoulders, and they were grinning. That day seemed like a million years ago.

• • •

The next day Jackson awoke to find a strange woman standing over him. He rubbed the sleep from his eyes and realized she was Mrs. Pressman, an elderly neighbor. Mrs. Pressman was a cranky woman with thick glasses and an aroma of vegetable soup that followed her everywhere. Jackson wondered if it was her natural smell or if she was buying perfume from the Campbell's Soup Company. Regardless, it didn't explain why she was in his bedroom.

"Your father has left for work. He asked me to keep an eye on you," Mrs. Pressman replied. "I don't cook, clean, hold hands, kiss boo-boos, change diapers, or read bedtime stories."

"Mrs. Pressman, I'm eleven years old."

The old woman lifted her glasses and squinted. "So you are. Your dad gave me this to give to you."

She handed him a note. His father had scheduled out his day, minute by minute. He wanted Jackson to clean out the garage, organize the basement, clean Butch's doghouse, rake leaves, and trim the hedges. Apparently, being suspended was not punishment enough. Jackson sighed and got dressed. He'd start with the garage.

But when he opened the garage door, he found something other than old junk inside. All five of his teammates were waiting for him.

"You are a complete loser, bro," Flinch said.

"Who gets suspended in the fifth grade?" Matilda asked.

"It's all your fault!" Jackson cried to his angry teammates. "If I wasn't busy flying off to Egypt, I wouldn't be in this mess."

"Well, your inability to manage your life is not going to affect ours. Brand sent us here to train you," Ruby fumed.

"Train? I'm in deep trouble with my dad. I've got a list of chores a mile long, and if they aren't done by the end of the day, he's going to put me up for adoption."

Duncan reached out and took the list of work from Jackson. "We'll help you with this. Training is more important."

"What about Mrs. Pressman?" Jackson asked. "My dad hired her to babysit and she's going to notice if I'm not working."

"I've taken care of her," Heathcliff said, gesturing to the front yard, where they could see the old woman doing jumping jacks. Her eyes were spacey—Heathcliff had unleashed his teeth on her.

"If she has a heart attack, it's all your fault," Jackson said.

Matilda went first, fighting Jackson with a variety of silly weapons she found in the garage, including a bucket, a pogo stick, and some old Hot Wheels race car tracks. In the meantime, the others started on Jackson's chores. Jackson

38°53 N, 77°05 E

watched from the garage as Flinch stood over a pile of leaves and clapped his hands. There was a sonic boom and leaves were blasted into the neighbor's yard.

Despite their long morning together, only Duncan would eat lunch with Jackson.

"I get that I'm not good at this," Jackson said to the sticky boy. "I get that you don't trust me 'cause I used to be cool. I also get that I'm not the ideal member for the team. But why do you all hate me so much?"

Duncan blinked in bewilderment. "You truly don't know?"

Jackson shook his head.

Duncan reached into his pocket and took out a blue sphere. He pushed a button on its side and it began to spin. A moment later Jackson heard Benjamin's voice.

"What can I help you with, Gluestick?"

"Could you pull up some surveillance tapes of Nathan Hale Elementary?"

"Anything specific?" the computer asked.

"Yes. Show us the file labeled 'Jackson Jones.'"

There was a strange humming sound and then holograms appeared. This time, instead of a three-dimensional landscape, Jackson saw a square floating before his eyes. A moment later it flickered to life—showing video footage recorded in a busy hallway. Jackson recognized it as the hall where his locker was and quickly spotted himself in the crowd. The video was taken at the height of his popularity.

"You guys have been taping me?" he asked.

"Just watch," Duncan said.

Suddenly, Flinch walked down the hallway. Jackson watched himself knock the boy's books out of his hand so that they scattered all over the floor. Brett and the rest of his friends laughed.

Then the image jumped to another day when Jackson gave Duncan a wedgie. The image jumped again, and he saw himself tripping Matilda so that she fell to the floor. Then he saw himself tape a KICK ME sign on the back of Ruby's jacket. Then he saw himself dumping a soda on Heathcliff's head. The video went on and on, but it was always the same—Jackson tormenting nerds, his teammates in particular. He stuffed them in lockers, flicked their ears, forced them to kiss his feet, dipped their faces into the drinking fountain, pulled their hair, gave them wet willies, and put them into full nelsons. All the while, he and his stupid friends giggled like idiots.

"Do you see?" Duncan asked. "I have about twenty more hours of this if you don't get it."

Jackson was speechless. He didn't recognize the Jackson in the video.

"They hate you, Jackson, because you're mean. You think

you were popular, you think you were well liked, but you weren't. You were a bully."

There was that word again. Bully. Jackson remembered the events in the video clearly, but not the faces of his victims. They all melted into a single, awkward, misfit kid. Teasing nerds had been fun, a joke. He had never once thought of it as bullying.

"We all got our fair share of it," Duncan continued.

"But you guys are awesome fighters. You could have put me in my place easily."

"If we fought back, you might have been seriously injured, and it would have blown our covers as spies. But there's another reason why we took it, Jackson. It's because we know that what the popular kids have to offer the world is so tiny and unimportant compared to what the nerds will do. The dorks, dweebs, goobers, and spazzes that you picked on are the ones who will grow up to discover the vaccines, write the great novels, push the boundaries of science and technology, and invent things that make people healthier and happier. Nerds change the world. Kids like you and Brett, and that gang of lunatics you called friends—well, you never amount to much. Knowing I have a bright future helps when I'm pulling my underpants off my head.

"I don't hate you, though I do think you are way too arrogant for your own good. The others, however, hate your guts. I know Ruby resents you because Brand brought you in without discussing it with her. Flinch and Matilda think you don't have what it takes in the brains department. And Heathcliff, well, he has a special place in his heart for the hate he feels for you."

"Why?"

"You took particular delight in abusing him. He got the worst of it," Duncan said.

Jackson watched as the video showed him dragging Heathcliff down the dirty hallway by his feet. Ashamed, Jackson looked across the lawn at his teammates, and for the first time he wasn't annoyed that they didn't want to be his friend. He suddenly understood. He didn't deserve their friendship.

18

The Hyena sat in a dark corner of the lab with her laptop. She was busy working on her résumé and searching want ads for contract killers. She wasn't having a lot of luck.

"Mindy, may I have a word?" a voice said behind her. Startled, the Hyena spun around and found Dr. Jigsaw standing over her. Terror swept through her. Had he seen what she was doing? Was she headed for the fire pit?

"I think it's time to introduce you to Simon," Dr. Jigsaw continued.

"Simon?" she asked, quickly closing her laptop.

"Follow me," the doctor said. He led her up a flight of stairs into the glass-walled observation room that overlooked his giant satellite dish. She noticed that the henchmen and scientists below were assembling huge solar panels. Jigsaw pushed a button and an enormous television screen rose up out of the floor. It was as big as a wall. The Hyena rolled her eyes. Villains always had to have such big TVs.

A strange man with a skull mask appeared on the screen. He was the same man she had glimpsed in Jigsaw's helicopter.

"Hyena, my name is Simon. Tell me about Cairo," the masked man said.

Jigsaw turned to the Hyena. She stepped forward and nervously cleared her throat. "Um, when I got to Cairo there was a team of . . . well, they were kids, waiting for me. They were trying to kidnap Dr. Badawi themselves. The odd thing is, they didn't seem like goons or henchmen. It was like they were trying to protect her."

"They're called NERDS. They are quite formidable," Simon said.

"I'm sorry," Hyena said. "Did you say they were nerds?"

"Secret agents with incredible technology at their disposal. They are of little concern to us," Simon said. "Precautions are already being made to help with your next pickup."

"Next pickup?" the Hyena said. "I got everyone on the list. There is no next pickup."

"You're not the only one who screws up, Hyena. It appears Dr. Jigsaw has revealed our plan to an old colleague."

Jigsaw shuffled uncomfortably. "Someone from my past could cause some problems. It's a bit of a long shot, but I did

the math and there is a five percent probability that he could figure out our plan."

"That's a chance I'd rather not take," Simon said. "Hyena, I believe this is a job best suited for your talents. Find the good doctor's friend."

The Hyena sighed. "And kidnap him?"

The man in the skull mask shook his head. "No, my dear. You're getting a promotion. I want you to kill him."

Suddenly, the screen faded to black and the odd man was gone, but the room was aglow with the Hyena's smile.

END TRANSMISSION.

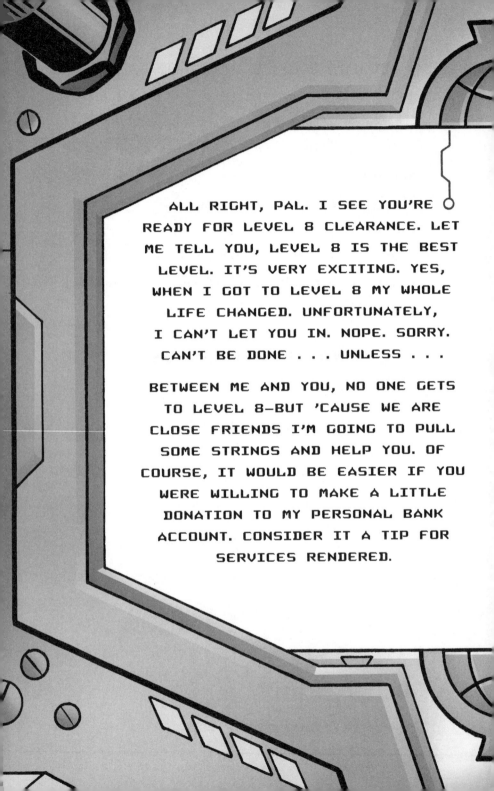

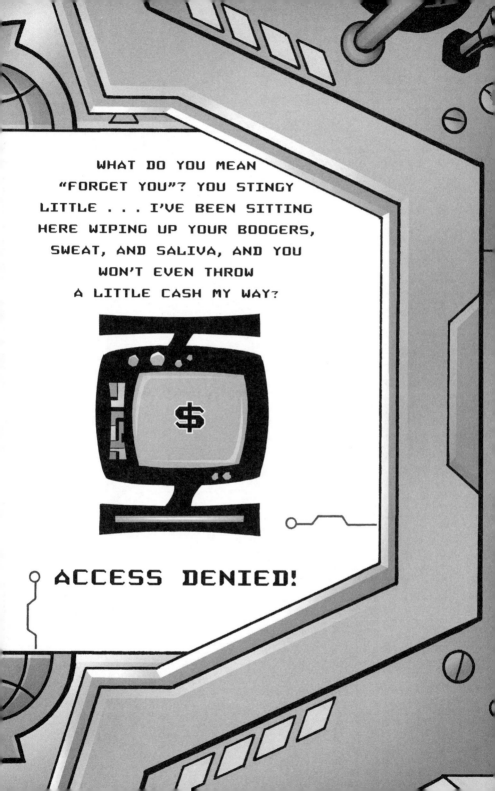

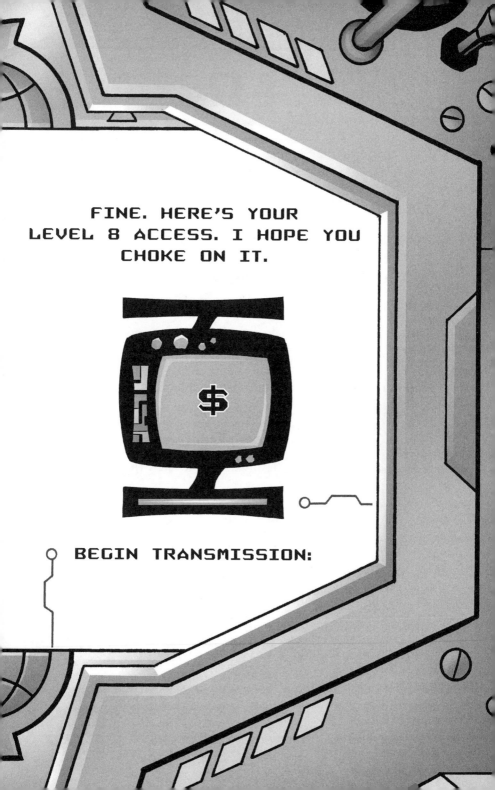

19

By the end of his suspension, Jackson's house was immaculate. The gutters had been cleared, the windows washed, and the shrubs pruned into the shapes of wild stallions. Jackson, with the help of Duncan, and the begrudging assistance of Flinch and Matilda, caught up on all his homework. There was even a moment when he was learning about past participles that they had all shared a laugh. He seemed to be breaking the shell that protected most of the team, though Heathcliff and Ruby still refused to speak to him outside of training.

When Jackson stepped back into Nathan Hale Elementary, he was feeling better about his life. The weight on his shoulders didn't feel so heavy, and he had a renewed determination to succeed not only in his classes, but as a secret agent as well. He had a growing sensation that nothing could get in his way.

He made it three feet when Mr. Dehaven appeared in front of him. "And where do you think you're going, Mr. Jones?"

"Uh, I was thinking class would be the first stop," Jackson said.

Dehaven eyed him carefully. "I've spoken with your teacher, and we have agreed that you shouldn't get a break because you were out for three days. So, you have quite a stack of homework to do and a quiz. I'd recommend you pass that quiz, son. It's worth fifty percent of your grade. Currently, your other fifty percent is a big fat zero."

Jackson nodded and hurried off to his class.

"Remember, Jones. Bull. Horns!"

Jackson made note of an interesting phenomenon in his class. When he took his mind off his former friends and his plans to regain his popularity, his schoolwork was easier. Crazier still—he was learning a few things.

In the halls he went out of his way to be friendly, especially to the kids he knew he had bullied. Most of them looked suspicious or stunned. Some refused to forgive him, but a few did. He even tracked down Stevie Lazar and helped him remove the crayons from his ears.

Then just as he was filling out his name at the top of the quiz Mr. Dehaven had warned him about, he felt a buzzing inside his nose that made him sneeze. He looked around and saw the rest of the team getting out of their seats. A moment later Heathcliff was putting the teacher into a trance.

"C'mon," Matilda said as they filed out of the class.

"That test is worth fifty percent of my grade," Jackson complained as he followed them into the hallway.

The others ignored him as they hurried toward the secret lockers.

"If I don't take it, I'm going to fail," he continued. "I'll have to repeat the fifth grade."

The team was still ignoring him as they all took their seats at the briefing table. Agent Brand and Ms. Holiday approached.

"It's good to see you, team," Ms. Holiday said. She seemed more chipper than ever,

"Yes, good to see you," Brand mumbled. He flashed a wooden smile, then looked over at the librarian. She nodded in approval.

"What's up, boss?" Matilda asked.

"I'll brief you on the School Bus," the agent said.

"Where are we going?" Flinch asked.

"Los Angeles," Ms. Holiday said.

"Los Angeles?" Jackson exclaimed. "We were just in Egypt three days ago."

"Welcome to the world of a secret agent," Flinch said. "I call shotgun!"

As the lunch lady piloted the School Bus into the stratosphere, Agent Brand and Ms. Holiday began the briefing.

"Team, your destination is the home of Hector Munoz," Ms. Holiday said.

A blue orb produced a hologram of a chubby man with thick black hair, a wide face, and plump lips. "This is him," Brand explained. "He's a theoretical mathematician."

Jackson had no idea what a theoretical mathematician was, but Duncan squealed and clapped his hands.

"OK, maybe I missed the day when we discussed theoretical math," Jackson said.

"Or maybe you're a dummy." Ruby rolled her eyes and received an angry glare from Ms. Holiday.

"Don't be afraid to ask a question, Jackson," Duncan said. "There are no dumb questions. Theoretical math is a field of study in which scientists use equations to determine what is possible, even if it is impractical. For instance, time travel is possible, but the amount of power needed to make a single trip would drain the planet of every last resource. In fact, you'd need at least a hundred more Earths to get the job done."

"Well, if it's impractical, why study it at all?" Jackson said.

Duncan seemed confused and Jackson suspected the boy was reexamining his belief about dumb questions. "Well . . . it's so we can know."

"Dr. Munoz wasn't on the list," Ruby said. "What does he have to do with all of this?"

"Uh . . . good observation," Mr. Brand said. He seemed to stumble over the compliment. "Dr. Munoz was a colleague of one Dr. Felix Jigsaw."

"The Jigsaw Puzzle King," Ruby said.

"You're familiar with the doctor?" Brand asked.

"Isn't everyone?" the itchy girl asked. "He's a legend in the world of competitive jigsawing!"

"Competitive jigsawing?" Jackson laughed. The nerds looked at him as if he were a soupy zucchini they found in the bottom of the crisper drawer. "You're not joking?"

Agent Brand continued. "Glad to know you have heard of him, Pufferfish. Er . . . you are a valuable member of this group."

"What's going on here?" Matilda asked Agent Brand.

"Pardon me?"

"What's with all the compliments? 'You are a valuable member of this group.' You never praise us!"

Agent Brand flashed another look at Ms. Holiday. "It has come to my attention that you are children and maybe I shouldn't be talking to you like seasoned war veterans. Thus, I'm trying to present a more positive tone."

"Did you put him up to this?" Matilda asked the librarian.

Ms. Holiday shook her head. "I have no idea what you are talking about," she lied. Ruby scratched her arm furiously.

Brand scowled. "If we can get back to Jigsaw. He's an expert on continental shifts in the Earth's surface. Apparently, he and Dr. Munoz worked on a variety of projects together before Jigsaw lost his mind and had a stay at a mental hospital in Minneapolis. Dr. Munoz approached the FBI when Jigsaw was in treatment. He claimed the man was building a machine that could move continents."

"No way!" Flinch shouted. "That explains Greenland and Hawaii!"

"Maybe," Heathcliff said. "Still, that kind of technology is pretty advanced. What tells us Jigsaw is smart enough to do something like that?"

"He's not," Brand said. "But when you look at the list of big brains that have been kidnapped recently—experts on geology and advanced power sources, inventors—he might be able to put something together."

"You think Jigsaw is behind the kidnappings?" Ruby asked.

Brand nodded. "And I think we've already met someone who is helping him."

The hologram changed again. Jackson saw a three-dimensional drawing of the blonde kidnapper he had come face-to-face with in Cairo. He was stunned by the details his teammates had re-created. It looked just like her, down to her dazzling green eyes. She was so pretty. Why did she have to be a bad guy?

"Meet Mindy Beauchamp," Ms. Holiday said.

The image was replaced with a photograph of a young woman wearing a sash and a tiara. The kidnapper and this beauty queen were the same girl.

"Otherwise known as the Hyena," Agent Brand said.

"Why do they call her the Hyena?" Ruby asked.

"We're still working on it," Ms. Holiday said. "But we do know a little bit about her. She's a former pageant contestant who gave up her sash and gown for life as a professional goon. She's been spotted at a few of the kidnappings."

"Bingo!" Matilda said as she cracked her knuckles. "Now I know who to punch in the face."

"That still doesn't explain why we're headed to Los Angeles," Jackson said.

Ms. Holiday nodded. "Dr. Munoz lives there with his nine-year-old daughter. When he approached the FBI, he claimed to have some of the schematics for Jigsaw's continental-shift machine, but they thought he was crazy, too."

"Can't he just mail them to us?" Jackson said. "I'm missing a very important test."

Agent Brand shook his head. "We've reached out to him,

but Munoz believes he's being watched and is refusing to talk. He won't even repeat what he told the FBI. So, the team is going to him for a face-to-face. Your cover will be his daughter Elizabeth's birthday party. You need to find the schematics and see if you can get Munoz to talk about Jigsaw."

"How do we plan on finding the documents?" Duncan asked.

Ms. Holiday reached down into a bag and took out a guinea pig. It had a big red bow wrapped around its belly. "With this."

"Guinea pig cameras rule!" Flinch cried.

The cockpit door opened and the lunch lady poked his head out. "We're over the drop point," he shouted.

"Not again!" Jackson groaned. "You know, you can land this thing and just let us walk off."

"Get your gear," Brand said, ignoring him and gesturing to six backpacks at the front of the rocket. Inside his, Jackson found a complete mariachi outfit: a slim black jacket and matching pants, a sombrero, and boots.

"What's all this?"

"Part of your cover. Munoz's daughter is turning nine today, and you're the entertainment. You're posing as members of the hottest young pop band in America, Del Loco."

"No way!" Flinch shouted as he leaped to his feet. His body

twitched and shook, and at first Jackson was sure the boy was having a seizure, but soon he realized Flinch was dancing. Then he started singing. "'Hey, pretty lady, don't walk on by—come and take a moment with the super fly.'"

Brand quickly cut him off. "Del Loco is an international sensation. They have coloring books, lunch boxes, their own TV show, and millions of records sold. Dr. Munoz had to pull a lot of strings to get them to play. Unfortunately, the real Del Loco is going to be detained at the customs desk at the Los Angeles airport. Ruby, you're on point as usual."

Ruby smiled briefly. "When our last director said I was 'on point,' that meant I was in charge. Is that what you mean?"

Brand gritted his teeth and looked as if he was swallowing a ball of impatience. He eyed Ms. Holiday who smiled at him and nodded. "Yes, I trust you," he grunted as if the words caused him physical pain.

"And me?" Jackson said.

"Observation only," Agent Brand said.

Jackson sighed as he strapped on his parachute.

"This isn't a punishment, Jackson," Ms. Holiday said. "You'll be in the thick of things as soon as you're ready."

The lunch lady opened the side door of the rocket, and a moment later Jackson was floating down to Earth. Duncan had given him some pointers on skydiving and felt confident he was ready to jump on his own. He landed in a bush, but aside from a few scratches he was fine.

While the others slipped off their parachute harnesses, Ruby began to give orders.

"Wheezer, can you get airborne?" Ruby asked. "I'd like to see if you can spot the doctor's house from here."

Matilda took out her inhalers. With one in each hand, she pushed the plungers and shot into the air nearly as fast as the School Bus.

"I've got it," Matilda voice rang in Jackson's head. "It's about a mile from here on foot."

"Good," Ruby said. "Flinch, why don't you run ahead and let Dr. Munoz know the band is on its way."

Flinch clapped his hands together, twisted the knob on his chest, and sped away, leaving a cloud of dust in his wake. Though he'd seen it before, this never failed to impress Jackson.

Duncan noticed Jackson's amazement. "He is incredible," Duncan said as they walked in the direction of the doctor's house. "He can lift nearly five tons and reach speeds of a hundred miles an hour if he's had enough sugar. And he's my best friend."

"He's such a little guy too," Jackson said.

Duncan frowned. "Size has nothing to do with it, Braceface."

"Don't call me that," Jackson begged.

"That's your code name. I'm Gluestick."

"I'm changing my name," Jackson said.

"Great, you need something more appropriate. How about 'Motormouth'?" Ruby said.

Jackson frowned.

"I like 'Railroad Track Boy,'" Heathcliff said.

"I know! How about Monkeybrain!" Ruby cried.

"What does that have to do with my braces?" Jackson cried.

"Nothing. I just think that Benjamin may have upgraded the wrong weakness. You're pretty dumb."

Jackson faked a laugh. "Hilarious," he said. "I'm being insulted by a bunch of kids whose greatest enemy is milk."

Soon they found their way to the doctor's home. It was a large adobe structure set back from the road. Inside, Jackson could hear music playing and children singing. A steady stream of caterers rushed in and out of the front door, carrying trays of cold cuts, tamales, and cheese. Flinch was speaking Spanish to one of them. The man nodded impatiently. Even though Jackson didn't speak the language, it was clear the man was busy and didn't have time to chat with a bunch of kids. He rushed off with his tray of roasted corn.

When Flinch spotted the team he rushed over. "He says the party starts in about fifteen minutes and Dr. Munoz is already wondering where we are. I told him we would be ready. We better get dressed on the double."

Just then a black van pulled up in front of the house. Several muscular men in dark clothes got out and began unloading colorful piñatas. Flinch took an interest in the piñatas and the candy inside, but could not convince one of the deliverymen to give him one for free.

The team entered the house and found a bustling beehive of activity. Some people hung streamers from the ceiling and others rushed about setting up tables. Nearly every surface had a plate of food on it. Jackson was starving, but Ruby would not let him eat. Instead, she ushered the team to a couple of back bedrooms to change into their costumes. The boys went into one and the girls another.

Duncan, Heathcliff, and Flinch raced to the far corners of the room. From his days on the football team, Jackson had changed plenty of times in front of other people and didn't give it much thought. He was nearly finished when he found a black wristwatch in his pack. It looked just like the one the rest of the team wore.

"I got a spy watch!" he cried as he slipped it onto his wrist.

"Try not to laser your face off," Duncan said.

After he admired it for a few moments, he noticed his teammates were still dressed in their regular clothes.

"What are you waiting for?" Jackson asked.

"A little privacy," Heathcliff said.

Jackson could see that Duncan and Flinch were wishing for the same thing.

"Let me get this straight. You guys have saved the world a dozen times since Monday, but you're afraid to change your clothes in front of each other?"

The boys frowned but then nodded in agreement.

"It's no big deal," he said, hoping to calm their fears.

"Don't presume to tell us that it's no big deal. Everyone in this room is seven hundred times smarter than you. We know what's a big deal," Heathcliff snapped.

Jackson felt like snapping back, but he remembered what Duncan had told him. Jackson had been very mean to Heathcliff. A memory flashed in his mind. The gym locker room . . . Heathcliff changing . . . Jackson snatching his clothes and tossing them into the showers.

Heathcliff grabbed up his clothes. "I'll find somewhere else to change." He stomped out of the room and was gone.

Jackson knew there wasn't anything to say. He sat down on the bed and pulled on his boots. He wondered if he would ever be able to win the forgiveness of his teammates.

There was a knock on the door and Matilda's voice could be heard from the hall. "You guys ready?"

"Just a second!" Jackson shouted, then turned his back. Flinch and Duncan hurried into their clothes and the three of them rushed into the hall. Heathcliff joined them a moment later. When everyone was assembled, they stood back and admired the outfits Ms. Holiday had collected for them. Each of them looked like a real mariachi.

"OK, let's go rock this party," Ruby said.

"Uh, one small problem . . . I don't play any instruments," Jackson said. "Not even the clarinet Agent Brand gave me for my fake marching band practices."

"We're a pop group," Duncan said. "We don't play instruments. We sing and dance."

"Uh, I don't sing or dance, either."

The team made their way to the backyard with Jackson reluctantly following. There they found a sea of partygoers. Everyone was laughing and excited, but when they saw the six mariachis they turned into an excited mob. People pulled at Jackson's hat and begged for autographs.

A man Jackson immediately recognized as Dr. Munoz approached. "You are late. Set up and get started."

Ruby nodded and turned to her group. She said quietly. "Let's sing a few songs, and then Flinch and Braceface will approach him."

"I get to do something?"

Ruby nodded. "I don't think you could screw up an interview with a witness. OK, let's give these people a show."

"Again, I don't sing. I don't dance," Jackson said, but he was pushed onto the stage anyway.

Flinch stepped up to a microphone. "*Buenos días*, everyone. We want to wish Ms. Elizabeth a *feliz cumpleaños*. We are Del Loco. Before we get started, we have a special present for Elizabeth."

A young girl stepped forward and Flinch set the guinea pig into her eager hands. She squealed with delight as a gaggle of her friends surrounded her. They each took turns petting the nervous creature.

"We hope you have a good time, and feel free to dance," Flinch continued.

Suddenly, a song blasted through the speakers. Jackson turned to find the team moving in a complex dance sequence. They were bouncing and hopping around like trained dancers while he stood on the stage like a dumb ape.

"Dance," Heathcliff said as he nudged him.

"I told you I can't dance," he cried.

"Just listen to my instructions," Matilda said, her voice ringing in his head.

"Left foot step to the right, now lunge, turn to the right and jump!" Jackson followed the best he could, which seemed to quell the anger of a group of young girls staring at him from the crowd.

"Spin on the right foot, spin again, pull back and thrust. That's it. OK, let's drive these kids into a frenzy. Braceface, grab that mic and sing."

Jackson looked at the others. "I don't sing." His voice bellowed out over the crowd. A moment later a burrito came flying out of the audience and hit him in the leg. Before things could get ugly, Flinch snatched the microphone and took over the song.

Everyone was dancing and singing and, best of all, completely fooled. Dr. Munoz and his daughter whirled across the dance floor doing a lively two-step. They looked as if they were having the time of their lives.

"Del Loco" played several songs before Ruby kicked Jackson in the shin.

"What was that for?" he groaned as he did a complicated swivel step.

"Look at your watch," she said.

Jackson eyed the watch. There was a flashing screen that read ACTIVATE GUINEA PIG. He pushed the button and the little screen was replaced with a video camera image. He could see dozens of little girls staring up at him and then realized he was seeing what the guinea pig was seeing. A moment later he watched as the girls squealed and the guinea pig made an escape. In no time at all it had scurried out of the backyard and into the house. Watching its point of view, Jackson saw it weave in and out of the crowd of busy caterers as it went from one room to the next.

Jackson continued his dancing and singing for several more songs, though his focus on the watch made him slam into Matilda during a tricky spin move. He accidentally kicked Heathcliff in the rear end, but finally the furry little camera stumbled into a room filled with file cabinets.

"That has to be it," Jackson said to himself. The watch flashed a button that said TARGET LOCK and he pushed it. At once a schematic of the house appeared, then a turn-for-turn map to the guinea pig's location.

Jackson and Flinch stepped offstage and hurried into the house. They found the guinea pig sniffing at a desk chair in a lonely room that overlooked the backyard and the party below. The room must have had twenty file cabinets in it, stacked up to the ceiling.

"This will take forever." Jackson groaned. "We don't even know what we're looking for."

"We better get started, bro," Flinch said. He tried to open a drawer but it was locked. He gave the knob on his chest a slight turn and then yanked at the drawer handle so that its lock busted. Then he did the same for Jackson's drawer. They sorted through files filled with bizarre mathematical equations and strange schematics, but none of them had Dr. Jigsaw's name on them or seemed to have anything to do with continents.

From downstairs Jackson could hear his teammates replaying a song they had already performed. In his head, Ruby's angry voice demanded they hurry.

"This is hopeless," Flinch said.

"Shouldn't you two be on stage?" a voice said behind them. The boys spun around and found Dr. Munoz standing in the doorway.

"We're not with the band. We're with NERDS," Flinch said.

"You're nerds?"

"Not nerds. NERDS. The National Espionage, Rescue, and Defense Society."

"But you're kids. You can't be older than ten!" Dr. Munoz cried.

"Actually, we're eleven."

"The government sends eleven-year-olds for this kind of work now?" Munoz said, shaking his head.

"Sir, we know you contacted the FBI about Dr. Jigsaw. We also know you have schematics for his invention," Flinch said. "It would be a great help to us—and to the world—to have them."

Jackson watched the man's face turn cold. "You're putting my family in danger."

"We're trying to help you," Jackson said. "If we can't stop that wacko, who knows where Los Angeles will be on the map tomorrow. Give us the schematics. You will be saving millions of innocent people."

Munoz shuddered. "Jigsaw will have me killed. The guy is certifiable! I worked with him for a decade. He was always odd, but as time went by he got worse. When he proposed his continent project to the board of directors, they laughed at him. He threatened the head of the program with a letter opener and was arrested. Scientists really need to stop laughing at one another—we're all very sensitive. Long story short, Jigsaw was fired the next day. I had to pack up his things, which I took over to his apartment. The entire floor was covered in this massive jigsaw puzzle. I don't think he knew I was there. He kept muttering to himself that he would never give up."

"Give up what?" Flinch asked.

"The reunification of the continents," Munoz said. "There's this theory that all of the seven continents—North and South America, Asia, Europe, Australia, Africa, and Antarctica—were once one giant continent. Scientists call it Pangaea. They think that shifts in tectonic plates caused it to break apart and drift to where the continents are now—but it's not my field. Jigsaw, however, was obsessed with it. He believed that all the world's problems could be solved if we just put all the pieces back together. He thought we should all be living next to each other again. I tried to explain what a nightmare putting them back together would be. Nearly every coastal city would be destroyed when the continental shelves slammed into one another. Millions of people would die. Moving land masses that large would create a tidal wave that would kill millions more. The natural paths of sea and wildlife would be devastated and wipe out a great deal of our food supply. Not to mention that his fundamental theory was flawed. Even if you could slide them together all nice and neat, people wouldn't get along any better. There are plenty of countries that neighbor one another now that have been at war for a thousand years. Jigsaw wouldn't hear it. He said the world needed to be put back the way it was meant to be."

Jackson glanced out the window. The doctor's daughter was in the yard. She was blindfolded and carrying a long stick. She swung it wildly at a piñata hanging directly above her.

"If he's so dangerous, you have to give us the schematics," Flinch begged. "If Jigsaw intends to use his invention, we need to know everything we can about it."

Munoz nodded in surrender. "Let me get them for you."

As Munoz rifled through a file cabinet, Jackson watched the party. The little girl had still not hit the piñata, though she had nailed quite a number of her friends. Finally, she was nudged as close to the piñata as humanly possible. She swung like a maniac and smacked two children, a caterer, a piñata deliveryman, and her own grandmother before she managed to bludgeon open the side of the piñata. A wave of wounded children rushed forward in hopes of snatching the candy in its belly, but something odd happened. The piñata, which was shaped like a horse, righted itself. Its two white eyes suddenly glowed red, and rockets popped out of its side. It took to the air and circled the crowd.

"Uh, my job is to observe and I'm clearly observing something very messed up," Jackson said.

Flinch stepped to the window and let out a gasp. "Pufferfish. Are you seeing what we're seeing?"

Jackson heard Ruby's voice crackle in his head. "Robot piñatas."

"Piñatas as in plural?" the hyper boy asked.

"Yes, there's a dozen or so flying all over the house. Something's coming out of them. OK, that's a missile launcher. Get everyone to safety!"

There was a terrible explosion, and the window Jackson and Flinch were standing in front of shattered.

"I've got to help the others," Flinch said as he reached into his pocket, took out a candy bar, and devoured it. "Braceface, your only job is to stay here and keep the doctor safe. No matter what happens, stay with the doctor."

"What if we're attacked by killer piñatas?"

Jackson never got his answer. The sugar was coursing through Flinch, and a smile spread across his face. He shouted, "I am mighty!" and a moment later he leaped out the broken window.

"My daughter!" Dr. Munoz said.

"She'll be safe," Jackson said. "There are six of us here. Just stay with me. The team will handle this."

"I'm going to get my daughter." Dr. Munoz raced out of the room, his files clutched in his hand.

"Dude, come back here!" Jackson cried out, but it was clear that the doctor wasn't listening. He scooped up the nervous guinea pig and shoved it in his pocket. Then he focused on Ruby's face. "Hello?"

Ruby's voice rang in his ears. "What is it, Braceface? We're kind of busy fighting evil candy containers."

"You told me to observe, so I thought I would tell you I'm *observing* Dr. Munoz running in your direction," Jackson said.

Ruby groaned. "Stop him!"

"So, you're giving me permission to get involved?"

Ruby roared.

"Good. By the way, he's worried about his daughter. If you see a girl carrying a stick, keep her safe. And do yourself a favor. Take the stick away from her. Jackson out."

"Code names only, Braceface."

"Stop calling me that," Jackson said as he raced after Dr. Munoz. He turned a corner and found the scientist cowering on the floor, files scattered at his feet, with a flying piñata hovering overhead. The machine's red eyes turned the dark hallway a creepy crimson, and its missile launchers hummed eagerly by its side.

Jackson stopped in his tracks. "Doctor, everything is going to be OK. I want you to get behind me. Whoa. Not so fast, just very calmly."

The piñata followed the doctor's every movement.

"OK, now, let's back around this corner," Jackson said.

Before they could take a single step, the piñata's red eyes blinked, something inside it started to whir, and smoke billowed out of its back. Before Jackson could react, it launched a missile straight for his head.

His braces swirled in his mouth, and in a flash they were morphing and twisting to create a large, round shield. The missile hit the shield, which deflected the blast and sent it back toward the robot. A moment later the robot, and most of the wall behind it, was on fire. Unfortunately, the files with the schematics inside went up in flames as well.

Jackson had no time to be upset. He dragged the doctor down the hall and out the front door. Unfortunately, another piñata was waiting on the lawn. Jackson could already feel his braces changing. A long lobster claw reached out of his mouth, grabbed the piñata by the neck, and cut it in half. The evil red light of its eyes flickered to black.

Jackson and the doctor moved across the lawn. "I have to save Elizabeth!" Munoz cried as he pulled away from Jackson. "I won't leave without her."

"Doctor, it's not safe here. The others are looking for her. I'm sure she's fine," Jackson said.

That's when the door on the nearby delivery van swung open and a certain platinum blonde goon stepped out. The Hyena had a grin on her face until she saw Jackson.

"You!" she cried. "What are you doing here?"

"Rescuing this guy from killer robots. Are these piñatas yours?"

The Hyena smiled proudly.

"He's under my protection, Mindy," Jackson said.

The Hyena scowled. "Does *everyone* know my name?"

"You'll have to kill me to get at him," Jackson said, mustering all his bravery.

"Hmmm," the Hyena said as she reached in the van and took out two silver sai with jagged points. "Well, I'm only being paid for the one kill, but a girl's got to do what she's got to do to get ahead."

She swung the sai at Jackson, but his braces swirled and out popped sai of his own. They blocked the blows before they could do any damage.

"We know you work for Jigsaw. We also know he's a nutcase."

"Everyone's a little quirky," the Hyena said.

She slashed at Jackson's shoulder, but his braces blocked the swing.

"He's behind the kidnappings, right?"

It was then that the Hyena flung down one of her sai and with her free hand threw a punch that knocked Jackson to the ground. While he was struggling against unconsciousness, he felt the goon stamp her boots down on his braces, preventing him from using them to fight back.

"He's building something, right?" Jackson sputtered. "Do you know what it is?"

"I don't get paid to know that stuff," she said. "I'm paid to kill people and you happen to be in the way."

"You have to listen to me. Jigsaw is building a machine that will destroy the world. He's insane, Mindy. He's going to kill billions of people."

"Not my problem. Now, where were we?" she asked as she pointed her sai at Dr. Munoz. "Oh, yeah, I was sent here to kill you."

Just then, little Elizabeth Munoz came racing around the

corner of the house. Tears were in her eyes as she attached herself to her father's legs. "Don't kill my daddy," she begged the Hyena.

Jackson watched the Hyena study the little girl. Instead of cold-blooded murder, he saw something soft in her eyes. He hadn't met any contract killers in his life, but he was sure they were supposed to have ice in their veins. The Hyena looked as if she might cry.

"I'm not going to kill your daddy," she said. "We're only playing, honey."

The little girl looked up into the former beauty queen's face. "Playing?"

The Hyena nodded. "We're playing Zorro. Your dad was Zorro. I'm the villain. He just threatened to take me to jail and I was about to run away. You know what? Why don't you and your daddy play now."

Elizabeth wiped the tears from her eyes. "I like to play imagination."

The Hyena lowered her sai. "I always did too."

She stepped off of Jackson's braces, and they slipped back into his mouth. Before he could get to his feet, the Hyena and her van were disappearing down the dusty road.

20

As the black helicopter soared
over the frozen tundra below, the Hyena reviewed what had
happened at Munoz's house, and she was not happy. For months
the Hyena had dreamed of the day when she stopped talking
about being an assassin and actually became one, but the kid with
the braces had ruined it all. She knew Jigsaw was a nutcase, but
had managed to find a way to tolerate the idea. What she couldn't
stand was a liar. Jigsaw's master plan wasn't about taking over the
world—it was about destroying it. She knew Jigsaw was building
some kind of doomsday weapon, but she had assumed he'd use
it to hold the world hostage. Mad-genius types never used their
weapons. They just tried to scare the willies out of people so
they'd cough up a ransom. But if what the kid had said was true,
Jigsaw was planning something so . . . so . . . so *diabolical.* Mass
murder was not why she had gotten into her line of work. Trained
assassins killed people one at a time.

When the helicopter landed at the fortress, Dumb Vinci was waiting.

"Is it done?"

She nodded.

Dumb Vinci grinned, revealing a mouth full of broken and missing teeth. "Good. I'll tell Jigsaw. Let's get inside."

She and Dumb Vinci rushed through the snow to the fortress. The wind was cold and vicious. It bit at her bare skin and she nearly knocked the goon down to get inside. Once there she excused herself and raced down the hallway to Jigsaw's enormous lab. The door was locked so she hurried up the flight of stairs and into the observation room that held his jigsaw puzzle pieces. Looking through the window to the lab below, she saw the satellite dish, still aimed toward the sky. It was attached to solar panels resting on short tables scattered about the room. Clearly, Dr. Badawi had been smarter than Dr. Lunich and had given Jigsaw instructions on how to build her supercharged power source.

"Beautiful, aren't they?" a voice said from behind her. She spun around to find Jigsaw, Dumb Vinci, and twenty hulking goons.

"Yes," she said. "Amazing."

Jigsaw smiled. "Putting the world back together takes some very beautiful and powerful tools, Mindy. My machine is perfect in both form and function, and I owe its existence in no small part to you. If it wasn't for your hard work, I could not have assembled the minds and tools to put all this together. The new world owes you a major debt."

"So you're saying I'm to blame for all the people you are going to kill," the Hyena said.

"Oh, you say it like it's a bad thing. Mindy, don't think of it as destroying the world. Think of it as putting it back together. It's broken and we're going to glue the pieces back together. In the beginning of our arrangement all I had was my satellite dish. I could use it to move major islands around, but I had no control. I might latch on to Greenland. I might hit the Galapagos. It was very random. Then you brought me Dr. Lunich and his amazing machine. The tractor beam is a marvel, and with a little adaptation I supersized it so that it now links to my satellite dish. This allows me to drag an entire continent wherever I want it. For years all my work seemed hopeless. How can you fix the entire world if you can't power the machine that puts it all together? That's when I read about the marvelous Dr. Badawi's solar panels. Now I have everything I need to put my jigsaw puzzle together."

"You've lost your mind," the Hyena said. "I never wanted to be a mass murderer."

"Harsh!" Dr. Jigsaw cried. His feelings seemed to be hurt.

"I was hoping you would want to witness it, but I guess I was wrong."

The goons cracked their knuckles and grinned eagerly.

"Getting rid of me is not going to be as easy as it looks."

Unfortunately, it was. The Hyena was completely humiliated as the goons hoisted her down the hall. They carried her into a strange, painfully cold room. It had no floor other than the sheet of ice the fortress was built upon. In the center of the ice was a hole big enough for a large man to slide through into the water below.

"This is my little fishing hole," Jigsaw said. "I come in here to think, and every once in a while I cast a line and do some fishing. I don't catch many fish, though. Actually, none. The water is deadly cold—about twenty degrees below zero. The average fish can't live in such temperatures. In fact, the average man can survive only about ten minutes in this water until his lungs begin to freeze and oxygen can no longer move through them. I suppose a young girl will last considerably less time. Oh, Mindy, I had such high hopes for you. I was going to give you a small part of Australia to rule as your kingdom."

"That's what they all say," the Hyena said.

"Drop her in."

The goons tossed her into the hole and she slipped under the water. She felt as if a million tiny ice daggers were ripping her flesh to shreds, and it took all of her concentration just to force herself back to the surface. Once she could breathe again, she gasped and shivered.

"Oh, look, we caught one," Jigsaw said. "Oh, I think she's too small. Toss her back."

One of the goons hoisted a block of ice off the ground. It was the exact same shape as the hole. He dropped it down just as the Hyena filled her lungs and forced herself under the water.

She reached up and pounded on the ice, but it was too thick to crack. In a panic, she swam away. She had no idea in which direction she was going, but she knew that moving would keep her alive a little longer. With each stroke she felt the ice above her for openings and looked ahead for any sign of light. Maybe if she swam out from under the fortress, she'd find thinner ice. But her fingers and toes were already feeling numb, and her arms and legs were getting heavy.

She continued her frantic swim until she saw a shimmering light above. She pounded on the ice with her fist, but it had no effect. What could she do? Then it dawned on her. She reached down, unzipped one of her new black boots, and pulled it off her foot. She thrust the sharp heel into the ice. A chunk drifted down to the abyss below. She struck again in the same place. Another chunk, this one much bigger, floated past her face. She hit the ice with all her strength again and again. She was wondering how much longer she could keep going when the last strike caused a crack. She pushed with every ounce of strength and found herself bobbing to the surface. Gasping, she dragged herself out of the water and fell into a coughing fit.

She had to get warm! She got to her feet and spotted the empty black helicopter. Hobbling toward it with her boot in her hand, she climbed inside and started the engines. A blast of warm air filled the cabin as she put on the headset and flipped on the propellers. She found a blanket behind the pilot's seat and wrapped herself in it. Then she eased the throttle back and the chopper was in the air.

"This little fish got away, Jigsaw," the Hyena said to herself.

She looked down at the boot in her hand. Its heel was gone, probably stuck back in the broken sheet of ice that had almost been her coffin. She wondered if anyone would notice if she started killing people while wearing sneakers.

21

Agent Brand paced the room.
His jaw was set like stone and his eyes were flashing. Jackson could tell his efforts to take a more "positive tone" had come to a screeching halt. Ms. Holiday watched him with growing anxiety.

"What happened?" she asked.

"We had an unforeseen incident," Ruby answered.

"You burned Dr. Munoz's house to the ground on his daughter's birthday," Brand said.

"Actually, the fire was started by the robots," Matilda said.

"Robots shaped like piñatas," Flinch said.

"OK, see, they were taken by surprise," Ms. Holiday said.

"On the bright side, Jackson saved his life," Duncan said.

Jackson beamed with pride. "The Hyena showed up," Jackson said. "It was the same girl who snatched Dr. Badawi in Cairo."

"So, Jackson, how did you get close enough to see this Hyena?" Ms. Holiday said. Brand was still pacing.

Jackson smiled. "I was protecting Munoz."

"You were told to observe!" Brand shouted.

Flinch cleared his throat and gave a twist to the knob on his harness. "I told him to stay with the doctor."

"And who told you to take him to see the doctor?"

Ruby stood up. "I did."

"And look what happened," Brand said as he slammed his cane on the desk.

Heathcliff shook his head in disgust. "There's no one to blame but Braceface. He made a tremendous amount of mistakes and he didn't follow orders. He's not one of us. He's never going to be one of us."

"That's not exactly fair," Duncan said.

"Fine. I'll prove it to you," Heathcliff said. "Hey, Braceface! Who's your favorite *Star Trek* captain?"

"Uh, Han Solo?"

"See, he's hopeless."

"OK, that's enough bickering," Ms. Holiday said. "Munoz is still alive and we got the schematics."

Jackson shook his head. "No, they caught on fire in the attack."

Ruby leaped to her feet. "See, Choppers is right. Braceface has shown the public his upgrades for the *third* time. He's not ready to be out there, and I don't trust his judgment. If you send him out again, I'm going to resign."

The room grew quiet.

"You really mean that, Pufferfish?" Brand said.

Ruby nodded.

Jackson couldn't be sure if Ruby was sincere or trying to push him out, but the worry on the team's faces when she threatened to quit spoke volumes. Pufferfish was much more important to the NERDS than some trainee who kept screwing up.

"Then clean out your locker, agent," Agent Brand said.

"No! She's not quitting. I am," Jackson said.

"No one is quitting," Ms. Holiday said.

"I'm not wanted here," Jackson argued. "You don't trust me, and you probably never will. Even if I did a good job, you guys would never accept me. Maybe I deserve it. I know I was a jerk before, but I'm not anymore. I wish you'd give me a chance . . . but you won't. So I give up."

He threw the words out there, wondering if anyone would argue. In his head he decided that if one person came to his defense, he would stay, but the room was quiet.

He looked at Duncan, but the boy wouldn't return his gaze.

"Take the braces and the computer chip out. I'm not one of you," he said at last.

Ms. Holiday looked at Agent Brand. The former spy was

leaning on his cane and rubbing his face with his free hand. He looked disgusted and disappointed. He shot Ruby an angry look, then nodded his approval. "Do it."

Ms. Holiday bit her lower lip and gestured for Jackson to follow her. She led him into the room with the upgrade chair and strapped him to the table. She started to tear up and wiped the corners of her eyes with her cardigan sweater.

"I'm truly sorry, Jackson. I don't think it's fair. You're doing as well, if not better, in the training than anyone on the team. Your time avoiding Duncan's tetherball is a record."

"Really? They never told me." Jackson said.

"Oh, and that man!" the librarian raged. "He told me he'd try to be more understanding. I told him, 'They're kids, Alexander. You have to talk to them like they're kids,' but he's as hardheaded as Ruby."

"I appreciate everything you've done, Ms. Holiday," Jackson said.

The librarian nodded, then pushed a number of buttons on the podium. A second later, Jackson was scooped into the chair. Ms. Holiday held his hand while the machine went about removing the nanotechnology from his mouth. It didn't hurt nearly as much as it had when it was implanted, with the exception of taking out his nose bug. The lunch lady had to use a long pair of pliers to yank it out.

When all of the technology was removed, Ms. Holiday escorted him through the Playground to the tubes that led to the secret lockers. Agent Brand was waiting for him by the exit with an outstretched hand.

"I'm sorry this didn't work out, son," he said.

Jackson nodded. He turned and looked at the Playground for what he assumed would be the very last time. Duncan, Flinch, and Matilda stood nearby looking on. When they realized he had seen them, they tumbled over themselves to hide.

"A few of them will miss you," Ms. Holiday said. "Even if they won't say it to your face. I'll miss you too."

"This is for the best," Jackson said as he pushed a button on the wall. The tube opened and he stepped inside. Jackson shot up and tumbled into the halls of the school, just as Brett and a group of his former friends walked past.

"Hey, loser," they said.

Jackson didn't argue. For once, Brett Bealer was right.

Sadly, losing his role in the team did not make Jackson's life any easier. He found it impossible to slip back into the routine of school. Nathan Hale Elementary was now far too distracting. It was brimming with secrets, and Jackson couldn't help but look for them. Every fire drill or pep assembly meant that something exciting was happening, and Jackson was no longer a part of it.

The team treated him like he was invisible. Even the lunch lady turned a cold shoulder to Jackson. It was difficult to have such exciting memories and no one to share them with.

One afternoon Jackson stepped into Mr. Pfeiffer's class and noticed that the NERDS were missing. Jackson didn't think much about it at first, assuming the team was on a mission. But the next day they didn't come to school, either. On the third day he wondered if everything was all right, but Mr. Brand and Ms. Holiday weren't around to ask. He was about to march right into the Playground for answers when he was confronted by Mr. Dehaven.

"Mr. Jones, just the man I was looking for," the stocky little man said. He clamped his hand down on Jackson's arm and dragged him down the hallway to his office. There Jackson found his father.

"Jackson, I am so disappointed," his father said.

"What's wrong?"

"Mr. Jones, do you recall a certain test you had to take in Mr. Pfeiffer's classroom last week?"

Jackson's heart sank. He had completely forgotten about the test.

"Today I got the results of that test. It appears you failed. In fact, not only did you fail, but you got a zero. Do you recall how much of a percentage this test was worth for your final grade?"

"Fifty percent," Jackson mumbled.

"And you got a zero." He turned to Jackson's father. "Mr. Jones, I've seen a million children like your son, and I have to say I'm concerned for his future. He lacks a certain level of dedication and ambition. Sad, because I'm told you were a first-class athlete and well liked when you were a student here."

"Grades were never my thing," Jackson's father mumbled as if it were his fault Jackson was failing.

Dehaven ignored the comment. "Luckily, there's a remedy for this behavior. Your son is going to repeat the fifth grade."

"He flunked?" Mr. Jones exclaimed. "It's only October!"

"Yes, I'm afraid he has," Dehaven replied. "There's nothing he can do to get back on track now."

"Jackson, what is going on with you?" his father asked.

"Nothing."

"Don't lie to me. I'm your father. Tell me what's going on," he demanded.

"Fine!" Jackson jumped out of his seat. "I was part of a secret agency that operates out of this school called the National Espionage, Rescue, and Defense Society, and it's made up of nerds. Each of us has enhanced abilities, and we tried to save the world from a lunatic. I was drafted right after

I got my braces, and I was training to become a full member, but I stunk, the other team members hated me, and I quit."

Jackson's father and Mr. Dehaven were speechless.

"That's what I've been doing," Jackson asked.

"If you only used that kind of creativity in your classes, you wouldn't be flunking!" his father shouted.

"Hey," Chaz said when Jackson got home after school. His older brother was wearing his gear and clutching a football in his hand. "Heard you flunked. What a dork!"

"I don't want to talk about it," Jackson said.

"Good, I don't want to hear it," Chaz said as he pushed his way past him. "Out of my way. I'm late for practice."

"Where's Dad?" Jackson said, before his brother was out of earshot.

"He's upstairs on the computer. He's looking up military schools to send you to," Chaz called back as he disappeared down the street.

On his way into the kitchen, Jackson noticed that his brother had left his helmet on the counter. He grabbed it and rushed to the door, but his brother was nearly at the end of the block. Chaz's coach would chew him out if he showed up without a helmet. Jackson raced down the street after him.

Chaz walked down Chambers Street and made a right at Beacon, which wasn't that odd, except his brother's school was in the opposite direction. Something was wrong. Jackson felt that old familiar tingle that told him he was about to discover a secret.

He continued down the street but kept a safe distance to make sure Chaz didn't spot him. Chaz went down Beacon, then made a left onto Hamilton Drive. There he turned down a nameless alley and stopped outside of a gated junkyard. Jackson watched his brother slip through a hole in the gate.

"What is he doing?" Jackson said to himself. He rushed across the street and peeked through the hole. He could see Chaz rummaging through the garbage. He found an old tin can and tossed it on the ground. Then he kicked it about the abandoned lot.

Jackson slipped through the gate and followed as closely as he could. He saw his brother plop down on the backseat of an old car and pull a paperback book out of his uniform pants. He leaned back and buried his nose in the story.

"Reading can be dangerous," Jackson said as he tossed his brother his helmet. "You might need this."

Chaz leaped to his feet. "What are you doing here?"

"What are *you* doing here?"

"Did you follow me?"

"You forgot your helmet. I was being a nice guy by bringing it to you."

"Thanks, now go home," Chaz demanded.

"You're not on the team anymore, are you?" Jackson said.

Chaz frowned. He kicked the car seat and then plopped back down on it as if in defeat. "I got cut."

Jackson's eyes widened. "They kicked you off the team? What did you do?"

"Nothing. I'm just not good enough," Chaz said.

Jackson sat down on the other half of the car seat. "But—"

"Everything's harder in high school," Chaz explained. "Everyone is good. I'm not special anymore."

"How long has this been going on?"

Chaz shook his head in disgust. "I got cut on the second day."

"So you've been suiting up every day and coming to the junkyard to read?"

Chaz winced and nodded. "After the look of disappointment Dad gave you when you got booted off your team, I just couldn't tell him. Sports mean so much to him."

"Oh, how the mighty have fallen." Jackson laughed. "We used to be the coolest brothers in Arlington, Virginia. Now look at us. You've become a reader and I'm pretty much friendless. I can't even get the nerds to hang out with me."

Chaz laughed. "I'm like a total nerd now. My only friend is Barney Tennant."

"Barney Tennant? You mean the kid who is always picking his nose in public?"

"That's him," Chaz said. "He's my BFF."

The boys broke into hysterical laughter.

"We're complete losers," Jackson said.

"We're so pathetic," Chaz agreed.

After a while the laughter faded.

"I've been a total jerk to you," Chaz said.

Jackson shrugged. "If it wasn't for your insults, I wouldn't have anyone speaking to me at all."

They talked for hours. Mostly about their father, but also about how much they missed their mom, and about how much their dad had changed since she died. They also talked about football and about the crimes they had committed against each other and the other kids at school.

"You know, if you really like to read, you don't have to do it surrounded by filth," Jackson said. "There's this place called the library. I've been in one. It wasn't that bad. The closest is on Henry Street, two blocks away."

"You're pretty cool for a little brother," Chaz said.

"And you're pretty cool for a big brother," Jackson replied.

"If you two hug I think I'm going to throw up," a voice said from above them.

Jackson turned and looked up. Standing at the top of a pile of junk was the Hyena. Her hair was like silver in the setting sun. If Jackson wasn't struck with overwhelming fear, he might have thought she was pretty.

"Who's this?" she asked, pointing to Chaz.

"I'm his brother," Chaz said. "Who are you?"

"I'm the—"

"Wait a minute!" Chaz said. "I get what's going on here. Is this your girlfriend, Jackson?"

"Uh—"

"Little brother! Hey, don't let me interfere with you two lovebirds. I'll catch up with you at home," Chaz said. He rushed to the gate, turned back and gave Jackson a raspberry, and slipped away.

"I've been looking for you," the Hyena said.

"Stay back!" Jackson shouted.

The girl leaped down in front of him. Instinctively, he swept her legs out from under her with his own and knocked her to the ground. A moment later he was running.

"Where was that move when you had to fight Matilda all day?" he grumbled to himself. He made a beeline for the gate, but before he could get there the Hyena had backflipped off a junked car and landed in front of him. He skidded to a stop and raced back the way he came. The junkyard was a maze of debris piled high in neat rows. Jackson raced down one aisle and made a quick right into another. The Hyena was right behind him every step of the way.

He knew his only hope was to try to make it back to the gate, so he made another quick left, then a right, then another right. He mustered every ounce of his former glory on the football field and sprinted toward the exit. It was so close. He just had to get there. Once he was on the street he could hide in the backyards of the countless neighborhood houses, and she would never find him.

And then he saw a blur to his left and felt something in front of his feet, and before he knew it he turned into a human tumbleweed rolling on the ground. He finally came to a stop on his back, gasping to replace the wind that had been knocked out of his lungs. Unfortunately, the Hyena was waiting. She tossed aside the mop handle she had used to trip him.

"If you're going to kill me, just make it quick," he groaned.

"I'm not here to kill you, dummy. I need your help," she said, reaching out her hand to him.

"Help?"

"Yeah, I need you to stop my diabolical boss and his evil doomsday device."

"Is that all?" Jackson said as he eyed the offered hand. "How do I know this isn't some kind of trick?"

"Why would I want you to help me stop the man who pays my rent?" she said. "I wouldn't, unless you were right all along. I don't want to know I helped someone destroy the world, and I can't stop him by myself. I need you."

Jackson took her hand and she pulled him to his feet. He dusted himself off, but kept a wary eye on her. "Why does a goon want to save the world?"

The Hyena snarled. "Watch it, pal! I'm not a goon."

"You act like a goon. You kidnapped those scientists."

"I was freelancing. I have to eat," she said. "Are you going to help me or not?"

Jackson shook his head. "You don't want me. You want the NERDS, and I'm not with them anymore." He turned and headed for the gate, slipping out the hole and into the street.

The Hyena followed. "What do you mean you aren't with them anymore?"

"I was a trainee," Jackson admitted. "And not a very good one. I screwed up a lot, so I quit. I'm out of the secret agent business."

The Hyena grabbed him by the shirt. "You can't just quit."

"You're not listening to me," Jackson said. "I *can* just quit and I *did* just quit. I can't help you."

"Then take me to the others," she demanded. "This is important."

"They're missing," Jackson said. "They've been gone for days. They're probably on some other mission."

"Listen, kid, if this wasn't the end of the world, I wouldn't have bothered. If you can't find your team, then it's up to you and me."

"Fine, but why are you wearing only one boot?"

The Hyena groaned. "Focus, you idiot. We have to save the world."

Even though all the students were gone and school had been closed for hours, the doors were still unlocked and Jackson and the Hyena stepped right inside.

"What are we doing here?" the Hyena asked impatiently. "Did you forget your lunch box?"

"This is our headquarters," Jackson said as he led her down the hallway.

"Your spy headquarters is in an elementary school?"

Jackson ignored her question. She'd be impressed by the Playground once she saw it. He had turned the corner heading for the lockers when a mob of panicked scientists nearly ran him over.

"What's going on?" he asked.

"End-of-the-world stuff, kid!" one shouted back to him.

"C'mon," Jackson said to the Hyena, and the two ran the way the scientists had come. Jackson shoved the would-be assassin into one of the lockers and slammed the door before she could ask him to explain, then climbed into his own. A moment later they tumbled out into the Playground.

There Jackson found Ms. Holiday shouting directions at dozens of scientists who were working furiously on computers.

"Find that signal!" she shouted. "I don't care if it bounced off every satellite in space. Find its origin."

Jackson was surprised by her tone, but even more surprised by her appearance. Gone were the cardigan sweaters and pleated skirts she usually wore. Now she was wearing a black bodysuit and a black beret, and had weapons strapped around her waist.

"Jackson, what are you doing here? And who is she?"

"This is the Hyena," he said. "She needs our help. Dr. Felix Jigsaw is going to destroy the world."

"We know," the librarian said, just as a scientist approached her with a map. "What?"

"My math shows that Australia has indeed moved. It was

here," the scientist said, circling the continent with a red pen then circling a spot in the ocean off the eastern coast of Africa. "Now it's here."

"Where's the team?" Jackson said. "They need to stop this now."

"Unfortunately, that is no longer an option," Ms. Holiday said.

"What? Why?"

"Benjamin, can you explain?" Ms. Holiday said, and the blue orb on the desktop began to spin. Soon, the holographic Benjamin Franklin appeared before the frozen landscape of the North Pole.

"Approximately an hour ago, a beam of magnetically charged energy shot out from the heart of the North Pole," Benjamin explained as the North Pole morphed into the blackness of space. The sky lit up as the beam of green light shot through Earth's atmosphere and bounced off a satellite.

"It's Jigsaw," the Hyena said. "It's a tractor beam."

The image changed, showing the ray bending to connect with the ground near the Sydney Opera House.

"Three days ago we sent the team to stop Jigsaw," Ms. Holiday said. "When we lost contact with them, Alexander—I mean, Agent Brand—and the lunch lady circled for hours. Now we've lost contact with them too. The School Bus is programmed to return to the school if it is abandoned. It returned empty, and there's not much information about what happened. I fear the worst."

"What are you going to do?" Jackson asked.

"Jigsaw needs a huge amount of energy to power his tractor beam. So far he's been able to move just one continent, Australia. Benjamin studied the energy output Jigsaw's satellite dish released to move Australia."

Benjamin appeared. "I've calculated that it will take seven hours for Dr. Badawi's solar panels to repower Jigsaw's satellite dish."

"It gives us a small window of time before Jigsaw can move another continent," Ms. Holiday said. "I'm going to stop it from happening."

"How?"

"Follow me," the librarian said. She led them into the upgrade room, pushed a button on the podium, and brought the chair out of the floor. Then she climbed into it. "I'm going to get the upgrades myself."

"I'm afraid that can't be done, Ms. Holiday," Benjamin said when he appeared in the room.

"Well, why not!"

"The upgrade application is specifically designed to work on children alone. You are much too old for the process."

"But this is an emergency," Ms. Holiday said.

"I'm sorry, but it simply can't be done," Benjamin said.

"Put me back in the chair," Jackson said.

Ms. Holiday shook her head. "No, you quit for a reason, and I respect it. I'm not dragging you back into this. I'm going to find a way to stop Dr. Jigsaw with or without nanocomputers. The best thing you can do is take your friend and find someplace safe. If Jigsaw's plans succeed, the world is going to be a very different place by tomorrow."

Jackson knew what he had to do. "Well, why don't you walk us out?"

"What?" the Hyena cried. "You're giving up just like that?"

"He's right," Ms. Holiday said. "It's best if you leave this to the professionals."

The children followed her toward the door, but just as they stepped through, Jackson grabbed the Hyena and pulled her back. Then he slammed a button on the wall, and the door slid down from the ceiling, locking the librarian out of the room.

"Jackson, you open this door this instant!" she demanded.

"Sorry, Ms. Holiday, but there's only one guy who can save the team, and you know it."

Jackson leaped into the chair. Straps wrapped around his feet as Holiday pounded on the door.

"Are you sure about this, Jackson?" Benjamin asked.

Jackson nodded. "I'm sure."

"Commence scanning," Benjamin said.

A moment later lasers swept over Jackson's body.

"Physical attributes are above normal range. Continuing to scan for weaknesses."

"What is this thing doing to you?" the Hyena cried.

A blue orb began to spin on the panel in front of Jackson, and a moment later a holographic skeleton was floating before his eyes.

"Benjamin, I hate to be impatient, but can we skip this? Just give me the deal you gave me before."

"Very well, except there is one thing," Benjamin said.

"What?"

"Subject's code name?"

Jackson took a deep breath and let out a sigh. "Call me Braceface."

Machines dropped from the ceiling and wrapped around his body. Soon his mouth was forced open by rubber hooks.

He turned to the Hyena. "You might want to step back and maybe avert your eyes. This isn't pretty."

"Think pleasant thoughts," Benjamin reminded him.

"Oh, this is so gross," the Hyena groaned.

END TRANSMISSION.

WELL, WELL, WELL . . . LOOK WHO HAS COME CRAWLING BACK FOR SECURITY CLEARANCE. YOU HAVE A LOT OF NERVE, BUSTER. WHY SHOULD I HELP YOU? WHAT'S IN IT FOR ME? YOU KNOW, THIS JOB DOESN'T PAY THAT WELL AND TIMES ARE TOUGH. YOU COUGH UP SOME CASH AND MAYBE WE CAN TALK.

NO, I WOULDN'T CALL IT BLACKMAIL. I'D CALL IT A BUSINESS OPPORTUNITY. YOU GET LEVEL 9 CLEARANCE AND I GET A LITTLE COIN IN MY POCKET. EVERYBODY WINS. YOU THINK ABOUT IT, AND WHEN YOU'VE MADE YOUR DECISION, TAPE SOME MONEY TO THE SENSOR.

THAT'S MORE LIKE IT.
I'M GLAD WE COULD COME
TO AN UNDERSTANDING. NOW,
LET'S GET PAST ALL THAT
UNPLEASANTNESS AND
MOVE ON . . . OH YEAH,
LEVEL 9.

ACCESS GRANTED!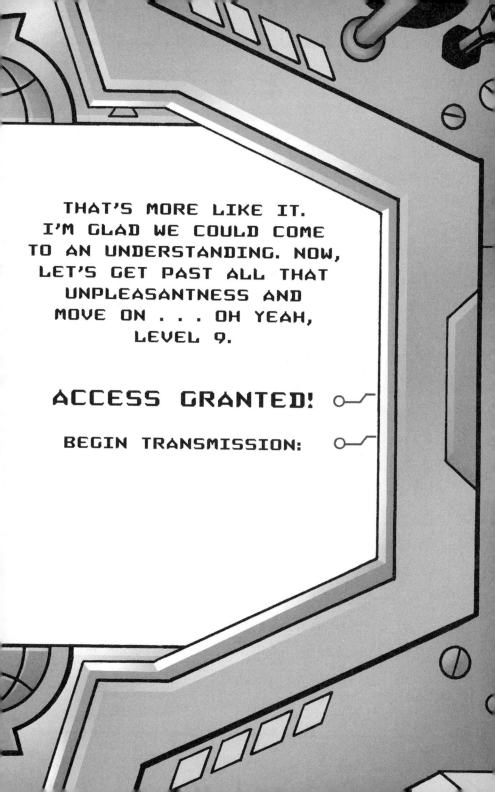

BEGIN TRANSMISSION:

22

Ten minutes later Jackson was on his feet and staggering through the door. Ms. Holiday was standing nearby. It was the first time he had ever seen her angry.

"I can do this, Ms. Holiday," Jackson said.

"I know!" she replied. "But I don't have to like it."

"I've got it," a scientist shouted as he rushed into the room. He was carrying a vat of something in one hand and a spoon in the other.

"I don't have to eat the creamed corn again, do I?" Jackson begged.

Holiday nodded. "You volunteered."

Jackson opened the lid and looked into the half-empty container. The slick yellow-gray substance swooshed around, releasing a noxious fume. It took all of his courage, but he dipped a spoon into it and shoveled a heaping helping into his mouth.

Jackson tossed the rest of the creamed corn to the floor and snatched the Hyena by the hand. "You ready to save the world?"

The Hyena nodded.

"OK, I have to make one stop."

Mr. Jones loved his dog Butch, but even he wasn't stupid enough to give him a bath. After several attempts and a few tetanus shots, he had devised a clever way to clean the dog and stay healthy. He pelted the dog with soap-filled water balloons and sprayed him with a hose from a safe distance. He had Chaz stand by as backup in case Butch got off his chain and wanted revenge.

Tossing the balloons also allowed him to have some fun with Chaz and to relive his glory days on the football field. Before he was injured, Jackson's dad was on his way to Ohio State University to play quarterback for the Buckeyes.

This evening, as he and his son tossed the balloons at the dog, he imagined himself marching down the field with the stadium on its feet. Just as they were getting the hose ready, they heard a roaring sound that seemed to be coming from directly above Mr. Jones. When he looked to the sky, he saw some sort of bright orange machine. He wondered if his imagination was playing tricks on him. But then a moment later the machine landed on the front lawn.

Astounded, Mr. Jones waved the garden hose as if it might

help him fight off the aliens that were invading the cul-de-sac. The door on the machine's side opened, and a metal plank lowered to the ground. A moment later his son Jackson stepped out, followed by a strange girl.

"Jackson," his father said.

"Dad, do you remember the breakdown I had in Mr. Dehaven's office?"

"Yes," he said.

"Well, it wasn't a breakdown. I really am a secret agent. Everything I said about my bad grades and being late and failing fifth grade was the truth. But I made a decision. You need to know what's going on with me, and maybe it's not going to be popular with my boss, but I'm not going to lie to you. I may have to lie to everyone else in the world, but not you."

"Jackson, this is crazy," his father said. "And perhaps you'd like to introduce your girlfriend to me."

Jackson's face turned bright red. "This isn't my girlfriend, Dad," he said.

"I'm actually a professional assassin," the Hyena said as she reached out and shook the man's hand. "It's a pleasure."

"Likewise," said Mr. Jones.

"Hey," Chaz said. She nodded back to him.

"So, we have to get going," Jackson said to hurry things

along. "The world is under attack. If we don't stop it, lots of people are going to die."

"What are you telling me, Jackson?"

"I'm going to be late for dinner," he said as he turned back to the rocket. The Hyena waved and stepped inside. Jackson followed. A moment later, the machine was blasting off once more.

"Uh, Dad? Since we're confessing things, I should probably tell you I got cut from the football team," Chaz said.

But his father was busy staring up at the stream of smoke rising into the heavens.

As Jackson and the Hyena came back down out of the stratosphere, they saw the icy landscape of the North Pole before them. Ms. Holiday had programmed the exact coordinates into the ship's autopilot program, and while they were airborne the kids took the opportunity to step into the cold-weather gear the librarian had provided. There was also the librarian's usual addition of home-baked cookies and thermoses of hot cocoa.

"Uh, you might want to skip the cookie," Jackson said just before the Hyena bit into hers.

"These are rock-hard. I think I might have lost a tooth!" she cried.

"She means well," Jackson replied.

The Hyena tossed her cookie against a wall, and it left a dent. "Here's what you need to know. The fortress is built like a huge tower and has dozens of rooms inside, but Jigsaw's lab is in the back. It's enormous and has an observation room that overlooks it. The kidnapped scientists are held in cells and watched by armed guards. Dr. Jigsaw has about a hundred goons and about five hundred henchmen on his payroll. There's not much in the way of security, but with so many people it's not going to be easy to slip in unnoticed. But I think—"

Wham!

Something hit the side of the School Bus so hard it knocked them to the floor. Their ears filled with sirens, and their eyes filled with flashing red lights. When they got back into the pilots' seats, they found the control panel was partially fried and sparks were showering over everything. A radar screen dropped out of the ceiling. On it were three angry red dots.

"What's going on?" the Hyena cried.

Benjamin's voice chirped through speakers. "It appears the ship is under attack. Three stealth warplanes are in pursuit. I suggest you take evasive maneuvers."

Suddenly, there was another loud siren screaming a warning, and the words INCOMING MISSILE appeared on a screen.

Jackson grabbed the rocket's throttle and pushed down. The jet jerked to a ninety-degree angle. The missile came within inches of the School Bus before slamming into the icy ground below. "These controls are sensitive," he muttered.

"Here comes another one."

Jackson banked left and the School Bus followed. Unfortunately, the missile followed him into the turn. He banked right and there it was again.

"I believe the missile chasing you is of the heat-seeking variety," Benjamin said.

"So what do I do?" Jackson asked.

"I suppose you should try to outrun it."

Jackson growled. "Thanks," he said as he sent the ship into a nosedive. The missile, according to the radar, was only seconds away.

"What are you doing?" the Hyena cried. "Pull up or you'll kill us."

"Relax, I've done this in video games a million times," Jackson said and kept the nose of the plane aimed at the ground. More warning sirens filled the air, screaming for him to pull up, but he ignored them as well. And just when it seemed like they would crash for sure, he pulled up and cleared the ground. The missile didn't have the same agility as the School Bus, and exploded on the ice below.

"I'm so awesome!" Jackson cried.

"Celebrate later," the Hyena said, and pointed to another missile warning on the radar screen.

The missile hit, sheering the right wing off the rocket.

"What's your next brilliant idea?" the Hyena said.

"Are you talking to me or the computer?" Jackson asked.

"Whichever one is going to get us out of this alive," the girl said, just as another missile slammed into the jet.

Bright red words appeared on the monitor. They read CRITICAL SYSTEMS FAILURE. ABANDON SHIP.

"OK. You don't have to tell me more than once," Jackson said. He helped the Hyena unbuckle her seat belt and together they dashed into the cabin. A panel above their heads slid open and two parachute packs fell at their feet. They helped each other into the gear, then rushed to the door. The wind outside howled and pulled at them with invisible fingers.

"You ever jump out of a plane before?" the Hyena asked.

Jackson nodded his head. "It's kind of become a regular thing these days."

She leaped out of the open door and was gone.

Jackson saw her drop like a rock and a moment later her chute opened. Jackson followed, and after several seconds of freefalling he pulled the cord on his chute and jerked as the fabric opened above him. It was bitingly cold, even through his gear, and his fingers quickly grew numb. But he had little time to worry about them. He heard an explosion, and saw a massive fire erupt on the School Bus. A third missile had slammed into the jet, and it broke in half like a child's toy. It plunged to the ice below.

When the ground rose up to meet Jackson, he fell over hard and rolled wildly, blinded by the snow in his goggles, until at last he came to a stop.

"Don't move a muscle," the Hyena said. He could hear her nearby but could not see her through his goggles.

"Can you believe it? We both survived," he said happily. He pulled his goggles off and brushed off the snow. That's when he saw what had triggered the Hyena's warning. Standing

over them was a mountain of fur and claws—a nine-foot-tall polar bear with glistening yellow fangs and coal-black claws.

"What part of 'don't move a muscle' didn't you understand?" the Hyena said.

"Uh, moving seems like a really good idea to me," Jackson said. "I think you're supposed to run from a polar bear."

"No, I think we're supposed to stare it in the eye," the Hyena replied.

"I'm sure that's a dog. What about jumping up and down and beating on our chests?"

"Gorillas."

"Fudge," Jackson said. "Well, I vote for running very fast!"

Jackson turned to the Hyena and grabbed her hand. The two took off at a sprint, but the icy terrain didn't make it easy. The polar bear, however, navigated the ground rapidly and with ease.

"We're not going to outrun this thing. It's fast," the Hyena said.

"Don't you have some kind of weapon on you? You *are* an assassin," Jackson said through gasps of the frosty air.

"Me? You're the superspy. Use that disgusting mouth thing of yours and kill it," the Hyena cried.

"I'm pretty sure polar bears are endangered," Jackson said. "It's illegal to kill them."

"It's trying to kill *us*!" the Hyena shouted.

But the polar bear wasn't their only problem. In their mad dash to escape, they were running straight for the burning rocket. The explosive heat coming from the wreckage was rapidly warming the ice around it. When Jackson finally noticed where they were headed, he realized he had to choose between two horrible deaths. So he stopped.

"What are you doing?" the Hyena cried, trying to drag him along.

"It's time to see what I'm capable of," he said.

The braces swirled in his mouth and morphed into a huge shield just as the bear reached them. The shield blocked the beast's deadly blows, and sparks flew off in all directions. The polar bear roared with anger and swung again—with similar results. The impact caused a little irritation to Jackson's teeth, but for the most part he realized he could probably defend them from the hulking animal for the rest of the day. "Problem solved," he bragged.

"Look!" the Hyena cried.

Jackson turned his head to see that the burning rocket had sent ribbons of cracks snaking through the ice they were standing upon. One of the cracks was fast approaching.

"This is just not cool," the Hyena said as the crack zipped between her feet. She stepped to the left as the pieces of ice began to separate. Jackson did the same. However, the polar bear was not so clever. The crack widened beneath it, and a moment later the big animal splashed into the water and vanished.

The pair now found themselves on a chunk of ice that had broken off completely from the rest of the sheet. The once-solid ice sheet was beginning to resemble a jigsaw puzzle. Worse, the ice was taking them farther and farther from Dr. Jigsaw's fortress.

Jackson's braces started to swirl once more and out sprang the four familiar spiderlike legs. He grabbed the Hyena by the waist, and the two rose into the air. The legs stepped over to the next chunk of ice.

"You know, this little gizmo of yours is very cool," the Hyena said. "But it's not going to help you with girls."

Jackson rolled his eyes and said nothing. He concentrated on the legs, willing them to step to the next block of ice. They were making steady progress, but unfortunately the chunks of ice were drifting farther apart. Soon they reached a gap that was just too far across for Jackson's metal legs to carry them over. He remembered Ruby's advice, about really focusing on his braces, and that he had control over what they did. He set the Hyena down on their chunk of ice and focused. His braces shot out of his mouth in all directions and wildly went to work assembling his vision. They morphed and twisted before his eyes, and when they were done he had built a small boat with an outboard motor around himself. The Hyena climbed aboard. No sooner was she seated than the boat started pushing through the waves toward the fortress. When they reached the solid chunk of ice near the fortress, their speed sent them skidding onshore.

"Tell me that wasn't cool," Jackson crowed as his braces slid back onto his teeth.

"Save the celebration for later," the Hyena replied.

"How do we get into this place?"

"Let us show you the way," a voice said behind them. When they spun around to see who it was, they were met with fists to the face. Jackson and the Hyena fell to the ground. Just as everything went black, Jackson heard his partner grumble two words.

"Dumb Vinci."

Jackson awoke on a lumpy cot under a bright fluorescent lamp. His head felt full of gravy, and his nose was running. Every joint in his body ached. He pulled himself up and waited patiently for his eyes to adjust to the blinding light. Soon, he could see his surroundings more clearly, though there wasn't much to see. He was in a windowless room with gray walls and a concrete floor. The Hyena was sitting cross-legged on the cot next to him.

"Good morning, sleepyhead," she said.

"Where are we?"

"Well, there's good news and bad news. The good news is

we are inside Jigsaw's fortress. The bad news is he has locked us in a back room and there's no way out. At least, no way I could find. You, however, have the superbraces. Why don't you use them to knock down the door?"

Jackson got to his feet but fell back on the bed with an awkward thump. He was still woozy.

"Easy, big shot," the Hyena continued. She got up from her cot and helped him to his feet.

They stepped to the door and Jackson studied it. There wasn't a doorknob—only a single metal panel. They opened it and found a tiny hole not even big enough for a key.

"OK, back up," Jackson warned. "This might get violent."

He focused his attention on the door, but nothing happened. His braces weren't swirling—not even a little.

"That's weird. My tech isn't working."

He scanned the room and spotted a bright orange device mounted on the wall. "What's that?"

The Hyena climbed up on her cot to eye the device closer. "This is an EMP transmitter—an electromagnetic pulse device. It shuts off electronics."

"That means no braces."

"So you're just a normal kid?"

"Aside from my incredible good looks and amazing athletic ability, yes. I'm totally normal."

"We've got to get out of here, Jackson," the Hyena said.

"Got any good ideas?"

She sat next to him. "Not a one. Some superassassin I turned out to be."

"Yeah, I know how you feel. I'm like the worst secret agent in the history of secret agents."

"All I ever wanted to do was kill people," the Hyena said sadly. "I'm going to be the laughingstock of the union."

Jackson smiled. "You say you're a killer, and you dress like one, but you act more like a hero to me."

"Just when I was starting to like you." She sighed.

"So, if you want to kill people, why didn't you kill Munoz?" Jackson said. "You had the perfect opportunity."

"It was his little girl. She loved him so much. They reminded me of me and my father, before he died," she said.

"My mother died last year," Jackson said.

"I'm sorry. You must miss her. I miss my father a lot. He used to call me Giggles," she said, then paused. "If you tell anyone that, I will murder you."

Jackson swore he'd keep her secret.

"He was a helicopter pilot—used to fly rich people around, and sometimes he'd take me. He taught me how to get one into the air. I was nearly as good as he was. But he didn't make a lot of money, and when he was gone there wasn't much left.

Our lives became about survival. We started entering beauty pageants to make money, but really they kept us just busy enough so that we wouldn't have to talk about him."

"Where's your mom now?"

"She moved from people to dogs. She won the Westminster Kennel Club Dog Show last year," the Hyena said. She sounded bitter. "She's got a West Highland white terrier named Daisy. You should see how she treats her. You would think Daisy was a person."

Butch flashed in Jackson's mind. "I think I understand."

"Ugh, we're becoming friends, aren't we?" the Hyena said.

"I'm afraid so," Jackson said.

Suddenly, the door opened and in walked Dr. Jigsaw.

"Am I interrupting something?" he said.

The friends were on their feet in a flash. "What have you done with my team?" Jackson demanded.

"Oh, you mean the NERDS and the dashing Agent Brand and the weirdo who dresses like a lady? Don't worry. They're safe and sound. In fact, they've got front-row seats to the re-creation of the world. Despite the fact that they came here to stop my plan, I'm taking pity on them and letting them watch the show."

"You're a screwball," the Hyena said. "You're going to kill billions of people for a silly jigsaw puzzle."

"You have no appreciation of order and beauty," Jigsaw said as a loud siren blasted Jackson's ears. "Oh, there's the alarm. My machine is almost ready to use again, which means it's time to put my *silly* puzzle back together. You two stay here. You don't get to watch the show."

Jigsaw left the room in a huff and slammed the door behind him.

"OK. We have to get out of here, now!" the Hyena cried.

"I agree," Jackson said as he got down on his haunches and peered at the tiny hole in the door. "But how are we going to get out of here? Think! I've seen those James Bond movies. How would he get out of this?"

"He'd use his laser watch or his exploding bow tie," the Hyena said. "You got either of those?"

"Not the tie," Jackson said as he tapped his watch, but it was as dead as his braces. "And the EMP is fudging the laser watch."

Jackson scanned the room for anything that might help. What he needed was something small and metallic, something that he could use to pick the lock. He went back to his cot and tossed the sheets and pillows onto the floor. Lifting the thin mattress, he spotted some rusty springs that might have worked, but were impossible for him to break off the cot. As he tossed everything back onto the bed, one of the pillowcases got caught on the end of his headgear. He tugged on it, but it was caught tight. Jackson unfastened the metal headgear from his bicuspids, removed the protective chinstrap, and tugged at the fabric until it was free. It was then that an idea came to him. Of course! His headgear might just be what he needed.

He bent the gear so he could get it into the lock. When he recalled how it had painfully twisted and turned his teeth, he felt an odd sense of revenge. When it was twisted into shape, he knelt down to the keyhole.

He had seen people pick locks on TV and in movies, but he had never done it himself. He wasn't sure that locks could be picked at all. Still, he had to try. He gingerly inserted an end of the headgear into the lock and jiggled it back and forth, hoping to turn the lock's internal machinery.

"Do you know what you're doing?" the Hyena asked.

"Not really," Jackson said. There was an odd click and he looked up at his partner. "I think I'm getting somewhere."

Then he was hit with a powerful jolt of electricity. It shot up through his headgear and knocked him backward across the room.

He tasted metal in his mouth, and his head felt like it had spent an afternoon inside a toaster oven.

"What happened?" Jackson asked.

"The lock must be electrified," the Hyena said as she helped him to his feet. "Here, let me try."

Jackson shook his head. "No! One of the things the team said about me was that I was worthless without the upgrades. They told me I lacked imagination and didn't use my brain. Well, they were wrong. I'm going to get us out of this room using my wits and my stubbornness. A little zap of electricity isn't going to stop me."

He snatched the fallen headgear off the floor and went back to work on the lock, only to have another powerful shock course through his body. When he picked himself off the floor, his hands felt numb and his whole body ached. Still, he returned to his task.

"Is this some kind of macho male thing?" the Hyena asked.

Jackson ignored her and continued to work on the lock. The following shock made Jackson bite down hard on his tongue. He knew he would feel the pain for days, but on he continued. The following shock made his eyes water and his temples hot. The one after that knocked him off his feet again. He lay on the ground, panting, frustrated, and feeling as if his very blood was boiling inside him. He fumbled with his headgear, doing his best to get a good grip with his clumsy hands, and jammed it into the lock again. He pushed and pulled, twisted and turned, all the while dreading the shock that would soon come, but he kept on probing, jabbing, turning, and then—*click!* Jackson stared in disbelief as the door swung open.

"Nerdboy, you rule!" the Hyena said. She cupped his numb face in her hands and gave him a happy kiss on the mouth. Then she ran into the dark hallway. It was his first kiss and he hadn't felt a thing.

23

Jackson rushed after his beau-
tiful partner through a series of dark hallways. He was just
beginning to wonder if she had gotten them lost when they
raced through a set of double doors into what appeared to be
an observation room. On one wall was a bank of windows that
looked out over an enormous laboratory. A laptop computer
sat on a desk, and there was a huge jigsaw puzzle spread out
over the floor. One glance revealed that it was a map of the
world, only with the continents crammed together into one
huge island.

"Look at this," the Hyena said as she stared through the
windows.

In the lab below, a gigantic satellite dish was pointed toward
the sky. At its center was a large rod that seemed to grow
brighter with every passing minute. Henchmen rushed about
running tests on the dish, and in the far corner a group of

scientists wearing orange jumpsuits cowered in fear. Jackson saw Dr. Badawi among them.

"Look!" the Hyena said, pointing to the other side of the room. There, with their arms and legs locked inside heavy silver balls, was his team: Heathcliff, Ruby, Matilda, Duncan, Flinch, Agent Brand, and the lunch lady. Jackson wondered why they didn't just use their upgrades to escape, but then spotted more of the bright orange EMP transmitters mounted around them.

"We've got to save them first," Jackson said. "Then we take out the machine."

"Not so fast," the Hyena said. "That lab is swarming with henchmen and goons. We're outnumbered. If we're going to save the day, we need to have a plan."

"I'm all ears," Jackson said.

"Me? I'm supposed to make the plan?" the Hyena said. She looked out on the lab one final time, then took off her boot. She turned the heel toward the glass that separated them from the lab below, and used it to carve a large circle. A circle of glass fell back into the room. Jackson heard the loud rumblings of the machine through the hole in the window, and could feel a strange and powerful vibration. It shook his internal organs and bones and magnetically tugged on his braces.

"Interesting footwear you have there," he said.

"Expensive, too," the Hyena said as she stepped through the

hole in the glass and onto a tiny ledge that ran along the walls of the massive lab. The ledge was a foot wide and there was nothing to catch them if they fell. "C'mon."

"C'mon where?" Jackson asked.

Impatiently, the Hyena pointed to a ladder that led down from the ledge on the other side of the enormous room. The ladder would drop them right behind the platform where the NERDS team was imprisoned. Knowing he had few options, Jackson slowly followed the Hyena.

"If we fall, it's going to hurt," Jackson said.

"Then don't fall. It would still feel better than getting zapped with one of those," the Hyena said as she pointed down to the floor. A team of thirty henchmen with huge weapons strapped to their chests marched into the lab. "Those guards are carrying microwave blasters. Instead of bullets, they shoot high-intensity microwave radiation. If we get caught in their sights, we'll be cooked like a Hot Pocket."

The duo did their best not to look down at the floor far below them. Every one of Jackson's nerves was tense by the time they reached the ladder and climbed down to the platform where the team was held.

"What are you doing here, Jackson?" Ruby asked.

"I've come to save your life and the world, if we get lucky," Jackson replied.

"And you brought one of Jigsaw's goons to help you?" Matilda asked.

"I'm not a goon!" the Hyena cried.

"She's very sensitive about the goon thing. Any idea how to get you out of these shackles?" Jackson asked, steering the conversation back toward the dilemma at hand.

"I've tried to break free but they're too strong," the lunch lady said.

"It doesn't matter," Agent Brand said. "If you free us, the team is helpless with those EMPs jamming their upgrades."

"How do we turn them off?" the Hyena asked.

"There's a control panel over there," Duncan said, turning his head toward the group of goons with the microwave blasters.

"You mean that tiny panel on the wall where the murderers with superweapons are?" Jackson complained, then turned to the Hyena. "Any suggestions?"

"Hey, I can't come up with *all* the plans," she said.

"The two of you should just go," Heathcliff said. "We're already in hot water. You're just going to make it worse."

"Heathcliff, I was a jerk to you and you're probably going to hate me forever, but right now I'm here to save your life."

"I'd be happy if you saved *my* life," Flinch said.

"I'll do my best." Jackson scanned the room and noticed two guards standing at the front of the platform. They had their backs turned to the hostages and hadn't heard a word of the conversation over the sounds from Jigsaw's noisy machine. "I've got an idea. Give me that boot of yours."

The Hyena understood what he had in mind. They tiptoed to the front of the platform, and Jackson brought the boot down hard on one guard's head. He toppled over unconscious, and the duo went to work on his companion. Then they dragged the henchmen back behind the platform.

In a flash they were dressed in the guards' clothing. The outfits were both way too big, but they rolled up the sleeves and legs and tucked in the pants. As they strolled across the floor, no one gave them a second look. They stepped right into the crowd of goons and stopped at the control panel.

"Hey, anyone know which button turns off the EMP machines?" Jackson asked.

"Yeah, it's the green button," one of the goons said without a second look.

"Thanks," Jackson replied as he slammed his hand down on the button. There was a loud siren and several flashing lights, and all the goons turned toward them.

"Hey! Who are you?" one shouted at Jackson.

"We're the people they sent to kick your butts," the Hyena said as she spun a roundhouse kick and caught one of the giant goons in the stomach. He hunched over and she brought his head down on her knee. Seconds later he was drifting into dreamland.

Jackson could feel his braces coming to life. They shot out of his mouth and slammed into the guards' jaws, one after another. The two of them made quick work of the thugs. Jackson looked back at his team. He guessed the person to watch would be Flinch, and he was right. The silver balls that locked Flinch's hands cracked open. A second later he was pulling his feet out as well.

"Let's knock some heads!" Flinch shouted, then banged on his chest like a gorilla.

"What's his story?" the Hyena asked.

"He eats a little too much sugar," Jackson explained as they ran over to his team.

"Flinch, free Choppers first!" Agent Brand shouted, and the littlest of the team did just that. Then he smashed the bindings holding Wheezer, then Gluestick, then Pufferfish. Lastly, he freed Agent Brand and the lunch lady. In the meantime, a group of angry henchmen with microwave blasters were heading their way.

Matilda's inhalers shot her into the sky, and she buzzed over the villains. They lifted their weapons to fire on her, but she circled them so quickly that in an instant they were blasting one another with microwave radiation. Their numbers went from twenty to five. Duncan stepped forward and grabbed the remaining henchmen's hands. A thick river of adhesive sprayed from his fingertips. They cried out in frustration when they aimed their blasters; their fingers were glued in place and they could not pull the triggers.

As Ruby looked on, her entire body began to swell and her skin turned blotchy and red. "There's more on the way!" she cried. "My allergies tell me there's at least a hundred."

No sooner had she spoken than doors at both ends of the lab flew open. Dozens of armed henchmen and goons raced in, firing into the air and barking threats. The lunch lady leaped off the platform into the fray, and with fists flying he pounded the men off their feet. Agent Brand wielded his white cane. He flipped it around, cracking the goons on their noses and slamming it into their Adam's apples. Despite Brand's wounded leg, Jackson could see what Ms. Holiday had said about him was right. He was the best secret agent the world had ever seen.

The Hyena and Ruby leaped into the fight as well. The Hyena's fighting style was elegant, almost like a dance. She kicked and punched with confidence and her opponents collapsed around her. Ruby, on the other hand, had an incredibly uncanny ability to *avoid* being injured. She seemed able to leap or duck out of the way of every attack. Jackson suspected she was allergic to physical violence. Many of the henchmen collapsed in exhaustion from trying and failing to beat her to a pulp. Others exposed themselves at the wrong time, and Ruby took advantage of the opening with a well-timed kick or karate chop.

"They're amazing," Jackson said as he looked out on the team.

"You took the words right out of my mouth," said Agent Brand, who was catching his breath nearby. "I . . . I couldn't get past their ages, Jackson. I felt like I was baby-sitting a bunch of high-tech crybabies but . . . they're as good as I ever was."

Jackson nodded. "Don't feel bad. I thought they were a bunch of misfits and losers. I guess we were both wrong."

The doors flew open once more, and a hundred more goons raced in with microwave blasters. There seemed to be an endless supply.

"Choppers, this would be a good time to use your upgrades," Agent Brand called to the bucktoothed boy.

"Yes, I agree," Heathcliff replied. He stepped toward the thugs, paused, and then turned back toward his team.

"What are you doing, Choppers?" Ruby asked.

"That's not my name," the boy said as he reached into his pocket. He took out a black mask and slipped it over his head. It had a white skull painted on the front and exposed his bright, ivory teeth. "My name is Simon, and what Simon says . . . goes."

"You're Simon?" the Hyena cried. "But that means *you're* behind all this!"

Duncan looked faint. "No!" he cried.

"Yes," Simon replied. "Well, of course I had help from Dr. Jigsaw."

Dr. Jigsaw and Dumb Vinci stepped through the crowd of henchmen, all of whom had their blasters aimed at the team.

"Heathcliff! Why?" Matilda said.

"Because I am sick and tired of this world, Matilda. It's upside down and inside out. Nothing makes sense. How else can you explain a world that cherishes charm and good looks over intelligence? How else can you explain a place where people are tormented because they are smart? Or because they don't wear the right clothes? Or because they can't fit their round bodies into the square holes? The planet is terrible, Wheezer. Especially to people like us. We're brilliant, creative people but we're treated like fools—shoved in lockers. Given wedgies. Laughed at. Things have to change. Luckily, my good friend Dr. Jigsaw thinks so too. Admittedly, we have different agendas. He wants to re-create a world that's long gone. I just want to smash it to pieces."

"You're as crazy as Jigsaw," Jackson said.

"If that's true, then it's all because of you." Heathcliff pointed an angry finger at Jackson. "You tortured me with your stupid pranks. You made me feel small and insignificant. My IQ is a billion times yours, yet you walked around like you owned our school."

"Heathcliff, I was a different person then," Jackson said.

"Maybe, but there's more like you out there. There's a million Jackson Joneses. Maybe billions, and the only way to stop them is to take their minds off picking on nerds and geeks. I'm going to give them something else to concentrate on—like the end of the world. Simon says turn on your machine, Dr. Jigsaw. Let's keep washing our hands of this whole stinking planet. North America next, I think."

Dr. Jigsaw climbed a small flight of stairs to a platform beneath the satellite dish. "This will only take a minute, Simon."

Jigsaw pushed buttons, and the machine's humming grew dramatically. There was a loud grinding sound, along with beeps and twitters. Then a green beam shot out of the top of the rod and zipped into the sky above. "It's starting!" the weird scientist cried.

"Stop this, Jigsaw," Brand begged. "You're killing yourself, too." The secret agent hobbled forward to stop him, but Dumb Vinci knocked Brand to the ground.

The tractor beam was at full power, and the room rocked back and forth as if it were on a stormy sea.

A huge video monitor rose up out of the floor and flickered

to life. It was set to a kids' puppet show, but that was quickly interrupted by an urgent newscast. A startled reporter appeared on the screen.

"We're joining you now live from the CNN newsroom. Reports are coming in of earthquakes in California, North Carolina, Yucatán, and Newfoundland. Another report just in to the newsroom claims that a massive tidal wave slammed into the North Slope of Alaska. We're going to check in with our meteorologist, Christopher Storm, to see if he can give us any insight on these incredible, almost simultaneous natural disasters."

The image changed to a nervous man looking over a computer readout. His face was pale and terrified. "Yes. First, I'm not really sure how to explain what is happening around the continent. These are phenomena like I've never seen, and I'm not sure there are words that would do them justice. What I can say is our satellites are telling us that North America seems to be moving. Again, North America seems to be moving. Now, there may have been some massive change in the tectonic plates, but I can't imagine what could have triggered it. For now, the National Weather Service is declaring a state of emergency for the United States. Canada, Mexico, and other countries are doing the same. Viewers are encouraged to stay in their homes. If you're on the street, there's a very good chance that you could die, so please, just stay indoors. Wait, I have some satellite pictures. Can we show them?"

Some images from space appeared on the screen. It was clear that they were tracking the movement of North America as it was drifting eastward toward Europe.

"I can't believe it," the weatherman said. "I just can't believe it!"

"Look at the destruction you're causing!" Duncan cried.

"I'm doing this for us," Heathcliff said as he turned his back on his former teammate.

"Destroy the beam!" Ruby shouted, and the NERDS rushed into action. Matilda fired concussion blasts, and Flinch punched the satellite dish with superpowered fists. But before they could do any real damage, they heard Heathcliff's voice once more.

"Simon says stop it!" he shouted.

And that's when Jackson knew things had gone from bad to worse. He looked over at his teammates. Each of them was in a deep trance. Their eyes glazed over.

"Kill Jackson Jones and the Hyena," Heathcliff said.

"Yes," they said in unison.

"Uh, if you can use those superbraces, now would be a good time," the Hyena cried.

The entire team attacked at once. Jackson tried to stop them. He turned his braces into a giant flyswatter and smacked Matilda out of the sky. Then the flyswatter morphed into a gigantic hand, scooped up some henchmen, and tossed them at Duncan and Ruby. Next the braces turned into a metal cage that clamped down over Flinch. Jackson was actually beating his own team of superspies, but the cage had been a terrible mistake. Flinch punched the bars, ripping a huge hole in them. The little nanobytes in Jackson's mouth swirled in agitation and slinked back onto his teeth. As his teammates approached again, he tried to activate his braces once more, but they popped and smoked. Flinch had damaged them, and now they were useless.

"I'm afraid we have a problem," he said to the Hyena.

"All right, I guess I have to do everything around here," she said as she reached into her pocket and took out a pair of earplugs. "Put these in your ears."

"What are these for?"

The Hyena frowned. "I have an ability myself."

"Like my braces?"

"Yes, and just as embarrassing. Put these in your ears and promise me you won't take them out until I tell you."

"Fine," Jackson said, though he was totally confused. He shoved the plugs into his ears and smiled at the pretty assassin.

"Happy? Oh, that's weird. I can barely hear myself."

Whatever the Hyena's plan, Jackson was sure he and the assassin would be killed at any moment by his superpowered teammates. But suddenly they stopped. Bewildered, he watched as one after the other began to smirk, then shake, and though he couldn't hear, it was clear they were breaking down into complete hysterical laughter. Jackson turned to his partner and saw that she was giggling herself . . . but not as uncontrollably as everyone else in the room. Jackson had to know what was going on so he took the earplugs out. What he heard was the most obnoxious, donkeylike, ridiculous laugh he had ever heard. It came out of the Hyena, and was so silly and stupid he couldn't help but laugh at it too. Soon his chuckle grew into a guffaw and the guffaw into a chortle and the chortle into a gut-busting, pain-inducing laugh. He was about to fall over from the pain in his side when the Hyena snatched his earplugs out of his hand and shoved them back into his ears. Her laughter disappeared, as did his giggle fit. He now knew where his partner got her name.

Finally, the Hyena removed the earplugs from his ears again. Jackson surveyed her attack. Everyone was on the floor holding their bellies—even Heathcliff and Dr. Jigsaw. Unfortunately, the green beam from the satellite dish was still blasting into space.

"If we're going to save the world, we'd better do it now," the Hyena said.

"But I don't have my upgrades." Jackson said. What could he do? He was just a kid with a broken pair of bionic braces. How did he get to such a point in his life? From star quarterback, to nerd with magnetized dental appliances, to secret agent in major trouble. And then it hit him.

"Help me get Flinch to his feet," he shouted as the two raced to the tiny boy's side. They helped him up and shook him until he stopped laughing and could concentrate on what they were saying. "Flinch, have you got enough juice in your harness to toss something at that machine?"

Flinch reached into his pocket and took out a box of chocolate-covered raisins. "I will! What do you have in mind?"

"Me," Jackson said.

Agent Brand staggered to his feet, still giggling, and grabbed Jackson by the arm. "Absolutely not."

"When you asked me to join the team, you said I reminded you of yourself, right? What would you do to save the world?" Jackson said as he turned back to Flinch. "Have you ever tossed a football?"

Flinch hoisted him off the ground with little effort. "Once. My older brother tried to show me."

"Imagine I'm a football," Jackson said.

"What are you doing?" Ruby cried.

"Ms. Holiday said the tip of this tractor beam is actually a giant magnet," Jackson explained. "I just happen to have a set of braces that are highly magnetized."

"You're crazy," Matilda said.

"You taught me that a good secret agent can use anything as a weapon," Jackson said. "On three, Flinch. Hut, hut, hike!"

The boy tossed Jackson into the air. He soared high to the very center of the satellite dish, with a wide smile on his face. The magnet in the tip of the rod tugged at his braces. The tentacles swirled out, whipping around wildly. They smashed at the rod, and soon the machine began to show signs of failure. The green beam of energy began to sputter. Jackson's obnoxious dental work was destroying Jigsaw's doomsday device.

"No!" Dr. Jigsaw cried.

Jackson looked down and saw Flinch pushing at one of the girders that held the satellite dish in place. He gave it a good shove with his shoulder, and it started to tilt over.

Now Jackson and the machine were falling, and there was nothing he could do to stop from crashing into the ground and probably dying on impact. Matilda flew to his side and tried to pull him off the dish, but she wasn't strong enough to break the hold of the magnet. So she used one of her inhalers to hover and the other to burn the rod holding Jackson in half. The magnet that held him fast came away, and Matilda flew Jackson to safety just as Jigsaw's doomsday device tumbled over. The mad scientist leaped out of the way, but his goon, Dumb Vinci, was not so lucky. His arm was caught beneath a jagged piece of the crumbling device, and he screamed in agony.

Unfortunately, this was not an end to the problems at hand. The dish crashed through the lab's ice floor and sank. The last ebb of the tractor beam hit the ocean floor deep beneath the fortress. As the beam exerted its pull, the icy ocean floor shot upward, forming an ice mountain that rose high into the air, taking Jigsaw's fortress and its inhabitants with it. In the midst of the cataclysm, the Hyena slipped and tumbled over the side of a rapidly rising cliff. She held on with all her strength, but when Jackson rushed to her, she was already slipping. He reached out and snatched her by the arm.

"Don't let me go," she said, looking down at the long drop below.

"I've got you," he promised.

"You!" a voice roared behind them. "You did this!"

Jackson turned his head just in time to see Heathcliff rush forward. "You, a complete moron, stopped my plan," Heathcliff said. He stomped hard on Jackson's leg, causing him to roll over the edge of the cliff. With his free hand Jackson snatched at the edge, holding on to the Hyena with his other hand. He felt like he was being ripped in two.

Heathcliff stomped down on Jackson's fingers, but Jackson

refused to let go. Still, he knew one more stomp from Choppers's boot would be the end of him and the Hyena.

Then there was a blur of movement, and Jackson watched as Heathcliff came sailing over the edge of the cliff. He screamed all the way down until his cries could no longer be heard.

Standing over Jackson was Ruby. She was scratching her scalp. "I'm allergic to betrayal."

24

Agent Brand and a team of scientists recovered the remains of Jigsaw's satellite dish. With help from Dr. Badawi and the rest of the kidnapped scientists, they managed over the course of several weeks to move North America and Australia back where they belonged. Innocent people were killed in the chaos and the property damage was staggering, but all in all, things could have been worse for the world.

Dr. Jigsaw's broken body was found on an icy cliff of the new mountain at the North Pole. Dumb Vinci's body was never recovered. Neither was Heathcliff's, though they did find his black skull mask floating in the icy waters.

"How will we explain it to his parents?" Jackson asked as the team assembled in the Playground.

"It's drastic, but the parents have been given a medication that will cause them to forget him," Agent Brand said. "It works much like Heathcliff's own ability."

Jackson was stunned. "So if I die on the job, my dad and brother will forget I was ever born?"

Ms. Holiday sighed. "I wish there was another way, but they would ask too many questions."

Jackson hung his head. "This is my fault."

Duncan shook his head. "No, Jackson, Heathcliff knew the world would change for him. As a grown man he could put all his days as an awkward kid behind him. He just didn't want to wait."

Agent Brand looked into the faces of his team. "You all did very well."

"Is that all?" Ms. Holiday prompted.

"I'm very proud to be working with you."

Before Brand could walk away, Ruby cleared her throat. "I think I can speak for the team—" Brand stopped in his tracks. "And say we feel the same way about you."

Brand nodded then walked out of the Playground.

"He's quite the chatty one," the Hyena said.

"We're working on him," Ms. Holiday answered.

Jackson turned to the Hyena. "So, did you talk to him like I told you? I think you'd be great on our team. I can't imagine what kind of upgrade Benjamin could give you for your laugh, but I bet it would be awesome."

"I did talk to him," she replied. "And he said no."

"I can't believe it. They wouldn't even have to train you," Jackson said.

"It's fine, Jackson," she assured him. "He offered me a job—doing something else."

"Really? What?"

"Sorry, it's classified, but—"

"But what?"

"But I'm not going to see you for a very long time," she said.

Jackson felt a crack in his heart.

"Don't be sad, Nerdboy," she said, kissing him on the cheek. "I'll be back someday. Maybe then you'll have those horrible braces off your teeth."

She turned and walked away. Jackson watched her step through the secret locker exit and disappear.

"Did she just kiss you?" Matilda asked.

"Gross!" Flinch shouted, his mouth full of chocolate and coconut candy.

"So, quarterback, how did it feel to save the world?" Ruby asked.

"No big deal." Jackson beamed. "I'm sure I'll do it again by Friday."

"Don't get a big head yet," Matilda replied. "You've got a lot more training ahead of you. I've got some great ideas about how to beat you up with a watermelon."

"So you want me to stay on the team?" Jackson said to them.

"Arghcheeww," Flinch said, then turned the knob on his harness. "Ah, you've kind of grown on us."

"It doesn't hurt that you saved our lives," Duncan said. "So, if you'll come back to the team, we'd be happy to have you, Jackson."

Jackson smiled and nodded.

Just then, the group let out a wicked sneeze.

"The signal," Ruby cried.

The lunch lady rushed into the room. "Agent Brand wants you out in the parking lot, pronto."

"The parking lot?" Duncan asked.

"Just go, children," Ms. Holiday ordered.

In no time, the team was outside. Agent Brand was aboard a real school bus. The lunch lady crawled into the driver's seat and beckoned the children aboard.

"What's happening?" Jackson asked as the team found their seats.

"Welcome to the TB-48 Orbital Jet," Agent Brand said. "Since we lost our rocket, Benjamin gave a real school bus an upgrade."

"Buckle up, kids." The lunch lady slammed a blue button on the dash, and the sound of grinding metal and moving parts filled the air. Jackson felt rockets blasting beneath him and watched as a wing extended from the side of the vehicle. A moment later the bus and the NERDS were blasting into the stratosphere.

Ruby looked over to Jackson. "Looks like you get to save the world again, Jones."

He smiled. "We're in the field, Pufferfish. Call me Braceface."

38°53 N, 77°05 M

25

THE FOLLOWING IS A
RECORDED TRANSCRIPT OF A
CALL INTERCEPTED BY NERDS
SATELLITE SURVEILLANCE
AND IDENTIFIED BY
FIELD AGENT THE HYENA,
A.K.A. MINDY BEAUCHAMP, AS
BEING BETWEEN SIMON AND
A GOON SHE REFERS TO AS
DUMB VINCI.

October 10, 09:15

Dumb Vinci: Hello.

Simon: It's me. I see you survived the explosion.

Dumb Vinci: Not quite. I lost a hand. I had a doctor
clean it up. They put a hook on it.

Simon: Cool.

Dumb Vinci: It actually hurts a lot and I have to give up the piano.

Simon: Oh. Your sacrifice is noted and appreciated.

Dumb Vinci: I'm sorry about the plan, boss.

Simon: (Laughing)

Dumb Vinci: Boss? Are you OK? It sounds like you're laughing.

Simon: Your concern is amusing, my friend, but completely unnecessary. You see, Jigsaw and his little machine were just part of a much bigger plan, one that is going exactly the way I want. Take care of yourself. I'll contact you when I need you again.

\<Connection is lost\>

EPILOGUE

Mr. Dehaven sat at his desk looking through the Nathan Hale yearbook. He was putting an *X* through Jackson's face and smiling when there was a knock at the door. It opened, and Jackson's father appeared.

"Hello, Mr. Jones, it's good to see you."

Jackson's father sat down at the desk. "Mr. Dehaven, I've come to you in hopes that you'll reconsider my boy's failure."

Mr. Dehaven shook his head in disapproval. "Absolutely not. Your son will have to repeat the fifth grade. It's for his own good."

"Mr. Dehaven, I was never a smart kid. When I was around Jackson's age, I got it into my head that my only chance at success was sports. Truth is, if I had buckled down and cracked a book from time to time, I might have been ready when I hurt myself on the football field. Luckily, Jackson's days as an athlete have come to an end early, so he has a real chance at taking a different direction before it's too late. And I think with a second chance he'll do it. Jackson is a hard-working kid. He's smart and has a lot of potential, and he's got his father's can-do spirit in him. And, to be fair, he has more responsibilities than most kids—more than you can even imagine. It's taken him a while to adjust but he's back on track. I couldn't be prouder of him, and I think that if you can let him move on, you won't regret it. He's a special kid. He's going to change the world."

Mr. Dehaven smiled. "Mr. Jones, Mr. Jones, Mr. Jones. Are you sure we're talking about the same Jackson Jones? The one I know is constantly tardy and disrespectful, and lacks commitment to his work. Listen, I appreciate you coming down here, but Jackson is a failure in my book and he's run out of chances."

"I was afraid you would say that, so I brought someone else who is hoping you'll reconsider," Jackson's father said.

Jackson's father put his fingers into his mouth and blew a shrill whistle. A second later, Butch raced into the room and came to a halt in front of Dehaven. He eyed the man and let out a low, threatening growl.

"I'll just let you two talk," Jackson's father said as he got up from his chair, walked out, and closed the door behind him.

Ten minutes later Jackson Jones moved on to the sixth grade.

The End

WELL, YOU MADE IT! I CAN'T
BELIEVE IT. NO ONE CAN
BELIEVE IT, BUT HERE YOU ARE.
THE REST OF THE TEAM HAS
ASKED ME TO CONGRATULATE
YOU. YOU'RE NOW AN OFFICIAL
MEMBER OF THE NATIONAL
ESPIONAGE, RESCUE, AND
DEFENSE SOCIETY.

THERE'S ONLY ONE MORE THING
WE NEED FROM YOU . . .

PLEASE ENTER
YOUR CODE NAME BELOW.

THAT'S IT.
THE BOOK IS OVER.
REALLY, THERE'S NOTHING
MORE TO TELL.

GO OUTSIDE AND PLAY.

YOU NEED SOME FRESH AIR.

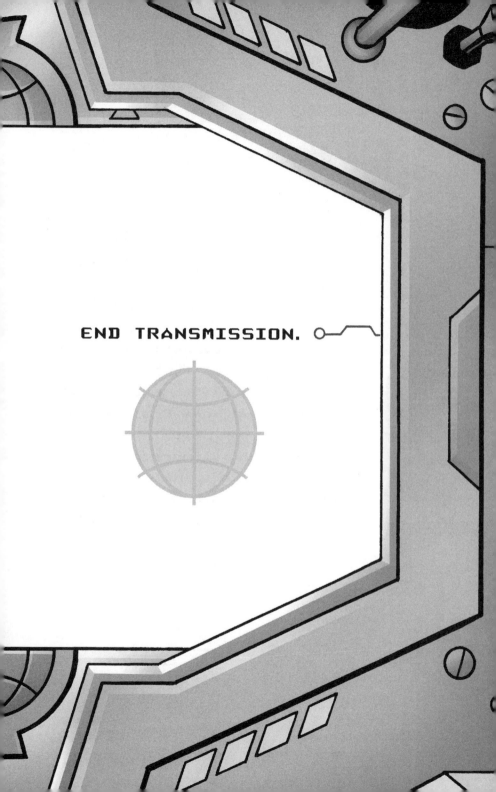

○ Acknowledgments

Many people helped me bring *NERDS* to life. Revealing them will put their lives at great risk, but I still feel they deserve a hearty thank-you. First and foremost, my editor, Susan Van Metre **(code name: Bookworm)**. Her imagination was just as important to this book as mine. I also want to thank my wife and literary agent, Alison Fargis **(code name: Brainstorm)**, who demanded that I write it. Jason Wells **(code name: Headliner)** deserves a lot of credit for his tireless efforts to get these books into the right hands. I'd also like to thank Ethen Beavers **(code name: Comicstrip)** for his amazing art and for agreeing to come on this roller coaster with me. Joe Deasy **(code name: Dr. Jeopardy)** continues to be an amazing sounding board, and much awe and admiration to Chad W. Beckerman **(code name: Masterpiece)**, whose inspired art direction produced a truly one-of-a-kind book. Special thanks to Howard Sanders and Lauren Meltzner **(code names: Hollywood and Vine)** at UTA. I also want to thank all the bullies who picked on me when I was a skinny, nervous kid. If it hadn't been for you, I wouldn't have hidden in the library and found my true calling.

About the Author

Michael Buckley, a former member of NERDS, now spends his time writing. In addition to the top secret file you are holding, Michael has written the *New York Times* bestselling *Sisters Grimm* series, which has been published in more than twenty languages. He has also created shows for Discovery Channel, Cartoon Network, Warner Bros., TLC, and Nickelodeon. He lives with his wife and their son, but if he told you where, he'd have to kill you.

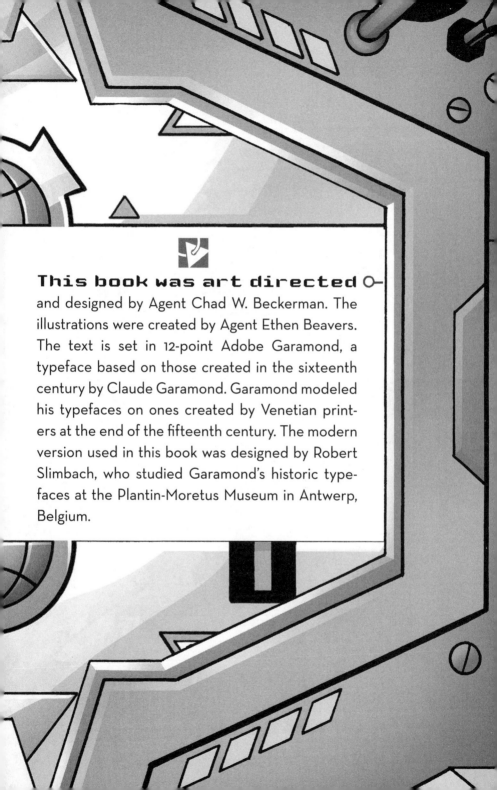

This book was art directed and designed by Agent Chad W. Beckerman. The illustrations were created by Agent Ethen Beavers. The text is set in 12-point Adobe Garamond, a typeface based on those created in the sixteenth century by Claude Garamond. Garamond modeled his typefaces on ones created by Venetian printers at the end of the fifteenth century. The modern version used in this book was designed by Robert Slimbach, who studied Garamond's historic typefaces at the Plantin-Moretus Museum in Antwerp, Belgium.

YOU STILL HERE?
WHAT DOES IT TAKE
TO GET YOU OFF
THAT COUCH?

FINE. I'LL GIVE YOU A PEEK AT THE NEXT NERDS CASE FILE. BUT YOU HAVE TO BUY THE REST!

M Is for Mama's Boy

By Michael Buckley

978-0-8109-8986-3 • $14.95 HARDCOVER

Simon's plan was *not* going exactly the way he wanted. He was trapped on a tiny ledge on the side of an enormous ice mountain at the top of the world—the North Pole, to be exact. The temperature was just above negative 35 degrees Fahrenheit, and in all directions there was little more than glaciers and drifting ice sheets. Firm ground was nearly a mile above, and the deadly cold waters of the Arctic Ocean were far below. He had been stranded on the ledge for two days, freezing, starving, and desperate for water. No, things were not going as planned at all!

Still, Simon (formerly known as Choppers, formerly known as Heathcliff Hodges) refused to ask his goon for a rescue. In his effort to become an evil mastermind, Simon had read many books, including one by business tycoon Donald Trump. It had argued that you should never let your underlings know you need help. It undermined their respect for you. No. He would save himself.

He pulled himself to his feet and balanced precariously on the tiny ledge. He searched the surface of the mountain for a handhold just as he had done so many times before, and once again he found nothing. Was he doomed to die? He went over everything he had ever been taught during his time as a secret agent. The NERDS headquarters was filled to the brim with gadgets that would save his life: grappling guns, antigravity sneakers, and much more. He had no gadgets with him. Right now he'd have settled for something as simple as a rope.

He thought of his former teammates, especially Duncan. He would be able to stick to the ice and climb to the top with ease. What good were Simon's huge front teeth when there was no one around to hypnotize? But what had the hopelessly incompetent Agent Brand said to the team? "You don't need gadgets. You are the gadgets." That was it! Simon was the gadget. He slammed his face into the ice, driving his enormous front teeth deep into the mountain. Alternately using his teeth and the heavy cleated boots he wore, he began to slowly climb the mountain.

Perhaps Simon should have been grateful for his amazing upgrades and his many hours of training, but that wasn't how he felt. He was boiling mad. Sure, being a member of NERDS had been exciting, but because the work was secret, when the young spies weren't out on a mission, they went right back to being picked on by their classmates. He and the others had suffered hundreds of wet willies, power wedgies, and flicked ears, but had they ever fought back? NO! They had to protect their identities and the work they did around the world. Well, it was all bunk! What was the point of having superpowers if you couldn't fight the bullies who tormented you? One day, while the school's resident meanie was dunking his head in a toilet, Simon realized that knuckleheads would always torment people like him. The only way to change it would be to change everything. He decided to destroy the world. With society in shambles, people would be forced to rely on those with great intelligence—namely, himself. Once again, reading and learning would be held in high regard and people like Simon would be admired rather than abused and humiliated.

But his brilliant plan had been foiled by his own teammates. Of all the people in the world, he was sure his former friends would join him. They were misfits, outcasts, spazzes—they'd been bullied, stuffed in lockers, and forced to hand over their milk money on a daily basis. But Simon had failed to see the effect Duncan Dewey had on the others. The chubby kid had always been a walking ball of positive energy. The abuse he suffered time and time again seemed to roll right off his back. And his grating optimism had infected the team. They acted as if Simon had betrayed them!

Simon's thirst for revenge kept him going through the painful climb, and after several hours he was close to the summit. At the top, he hoped to find the remains of Dr. Jigsaw's secret fortress, or at least some clothing and food. But when he was only a few inches away from the top, the mountain shook violently. He bit hard on the ice with what was left of his strength, knowing full well the source of the tremors. Jigsaw's continental-shift machine was still active and was forcing the mountain farther into the sky. There was another quake, and this time his teeth could not hold on. The next thing he knew he was falling—down, down, down into the sea. He hit the waves with a painful splash and, exhausted, he sank into the icy black abyss.

For Simon, death seemed immediate, but fate had another plan for him. It flash froze him like a fish stick. His heartbeat slowed to an almost undetectable rhythm, as did his brain function. Every molecule in his body crystallized, and a block of ice quickly formed around him, turning him into an ice cube of evil. For weeks he floated south with the currents, bumping into ice floes around Iceland and Greenland, drifting past Canada and right down the eastern seaboard of the United States. Several lobster boats tried to reel him in, but the block was simply too heavy, and by the time Coast Guard officials got there to investigate, Simon had drifted away. The cube shrank a bit as it bobbed along in the warm waters of the Florida Keys, and on down past Cuba. Eventually, what was left of the chunk of ice washed ashore on a tiny, uninhabited island in the Caribbean Sea.

The waves hurled it onto a pebbly beach where it was met by a squirrel with huge front teeth. Shocked by the cube's sudden appearance, the squirrel fled into the jungle and didn't return for three days. By then, the ice had melted considerably. When the squirrel mustered enough bravery, it hopped on top of the cube. It licked the ice and then spat the salty water out. Then, just as it was sure the ice posed no danger, nor any benefit, it peered into the crystal cube and saw Simon's giant buckteeth. It let out a startled squeak and then began to dig at the ice with its little claws. Its excited chirps brought dozens of squirrels out of the jungle, and together they scratched and chipped at the ice, attempting to free the boy. Squirrels are not big thinkers, as a rule, but if one had read the minds of these particular squirrels, one would understand that they thought they had stumbled upon their god.

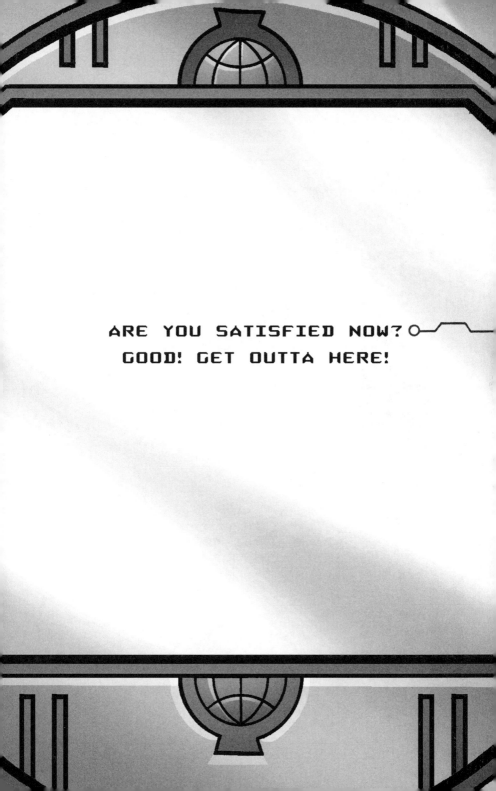

ARE YOU SATISFIED NOW?
GOOD! GET OUTTA HERE!

THE SISTERS GRIMM

1 *The Fairy-Tale Detectives*
978-0-8109-5925-5 hardcover
978-0-8109-9322-8 paperback

2 *The Unusual Suspects*
978-0-8109-5926-2 hardcover
978-0-8109-9323-5 paperback

3 *The Problem Child*
978-0-8109-4914-0 hardcover
978-0-8109-9359-4 paperback

4 *Once Upon a Crime*
978-0-8109-1610-4 hardcover
978-0-8109-9549-9 paperback

A *Today* **Show** Book Club Pick!

Amulet Books
An imprint of ABRAMS
WWW.AMULETBOOKS.COM

SEND AUTHOR FAN MAIL TO:
Amulet Books, Attn: Marketing, 115 West 18th Street, New York, NY 10011.
Or e-mail marketing@abramsbooks.com. All mail will be forwarded.

CATCH THE MAGIC—
read all the books in Michael Buckley's *New York Times* bestselling series!

5 ***Magic and Other Misdemeanors***
978-0-8109-9358-7 hardcover
978-0-8109-7263-6 paperback

6 ***Tales from the Hood***
978-0-8109-9478-2 hardcover
978-0-8109-8925-2 paperback

7 ***The Everafter War***
978-0-8109-8355-7 hardcover
978-0-8109-8429-5paperback

8 ***The Inside Story***
978-0-8109-8430-1 hardcover

Visit www.sistersgrimm.com today!

KEEP READING!

Attack of the Fluffy Bunnies
By Andrea Beaty
Illustrated by Dan Santat
978-0-8109-8416-5
$12.95 HARDCOVER

Hereville: How Mirka Got Her Sword
By Barry Deutsch
978-0-8109-8422-6 • $15.95 HARDCOVER

How I, Nicky Flynn, Finally Get a Life (and a Dog)
By Art Corriveau
978-0-8109-8298-7 • $16.95 HARDCOVER